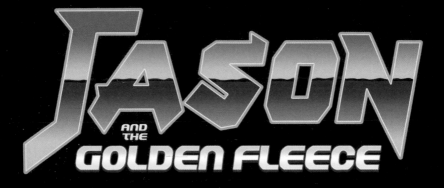

JASON
AND THE
GOLDEN FLEECE

RETOLD BY NEL YOMTOV

ILLUSTRATED BY GERARDO SANDOVAL
COLOR BY BENNY FUENTES

STONE ARCH BOOKS
MINNEAPOLIS   SAN DIEGO

Graphic Revolve is published by Stone Arch Books
A Capstone Imprint
1710 Roe Crest Drive
North Mankato, Minnesota 56003
www.capstonepub.com

Library of Congress Cataloging-in-Publication Data
Yomtov, Nel
    Jason and the Golden Fleece / by Nel Yomtov; illustrated by Gerardo Sandoval.
    p. cm. — (Graphic Revolve)
    ISBN 978-1-4342-1172-9 (library binding)
    ISBN 978-1-4342-1385-3 (pbk.)
    1. Jason (Greek mythology)—Juvenile literature. 2. Jason (Greek mythology)—
Comic books, strips, etc. 3. Argonauts (Greek mythology)—Juvenile literature.
4. Argonauts (Greek mythology)—Comic books, strips, etc. 5. Graphic novels.
I. Sandoval, Gerardo, 1974– II. Title.
BL820.A8Y66 2009
741.5'973–dc22   2008032064

Summary: Brave Jason comes to claim his throne, but the old king will not give up his rule
so easily. To prove his worth, Jason must find the greatest treasure in the world, the Golden
Fleece.

Creative Director: Heather Kindseth
Designer: Bob Lentz

Printed in the United States of America in Stevens Point, Wisconsin.
052012   006770R

TABLE of CONTENTS

INTRODUCING...

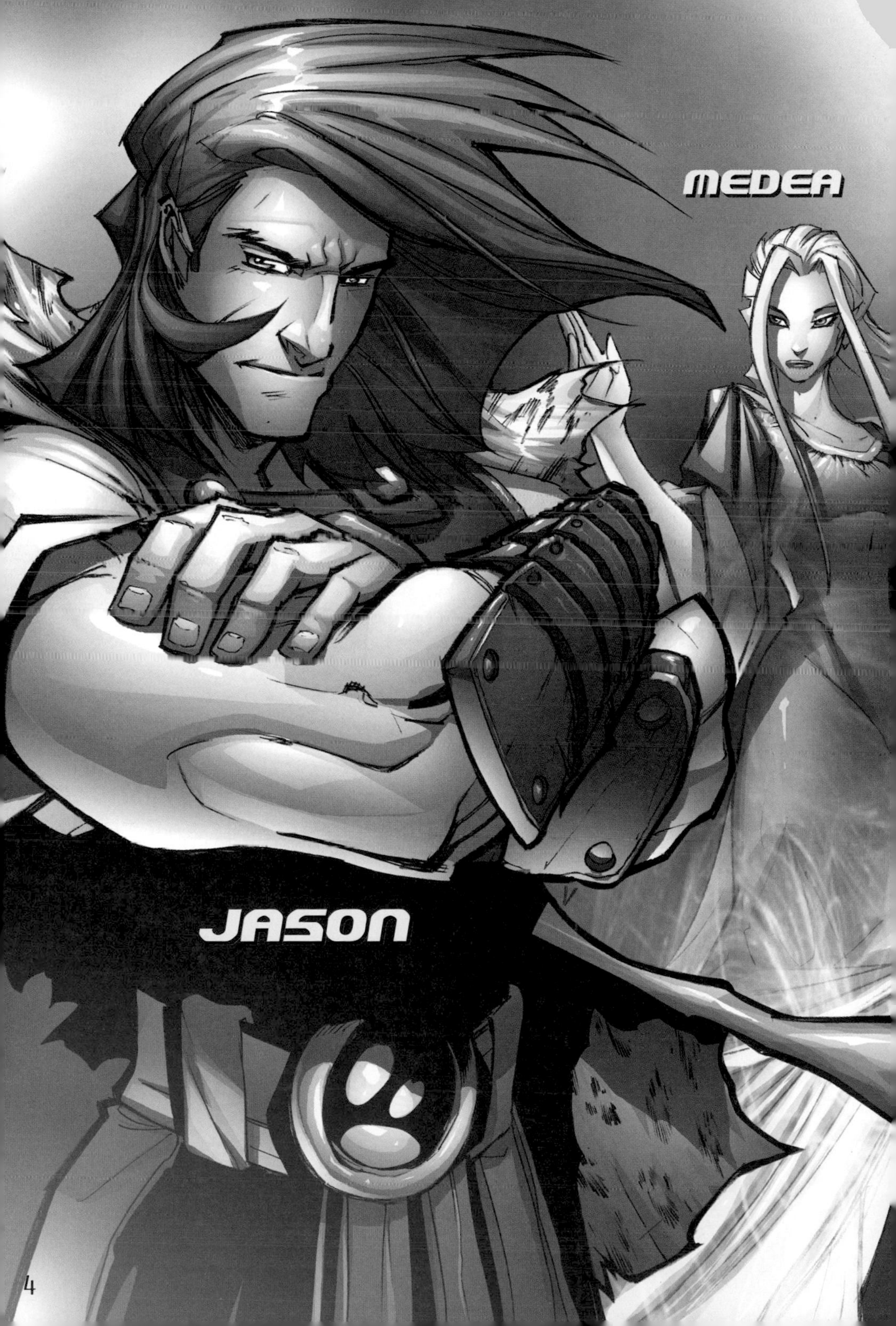
MEDEA
JASON

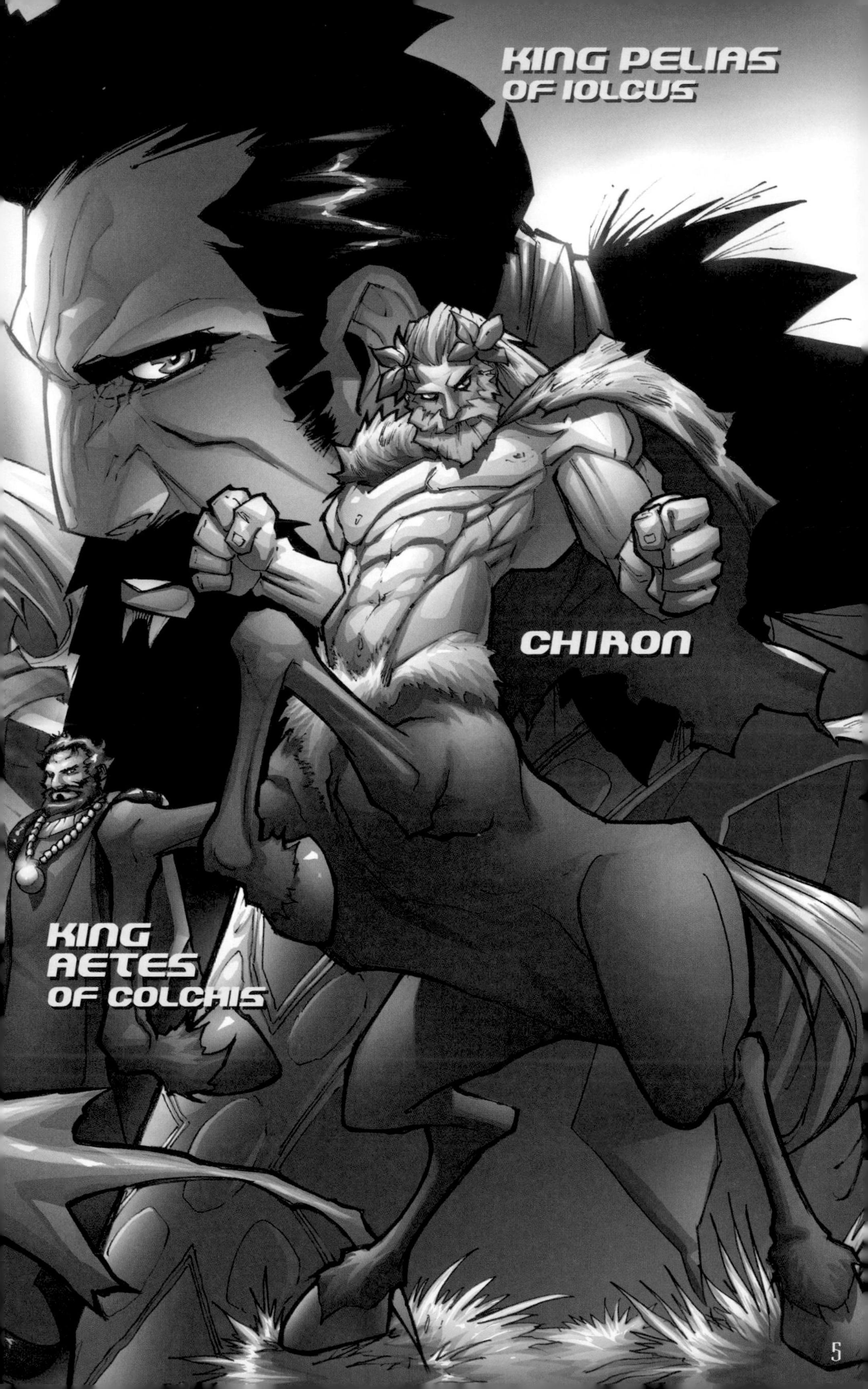
KING PELIAS
OF IOLCUS
CHIRON
KING
AETES
OF COLCHIS

CHAPTER 1: THE GOLDEN FLEECE

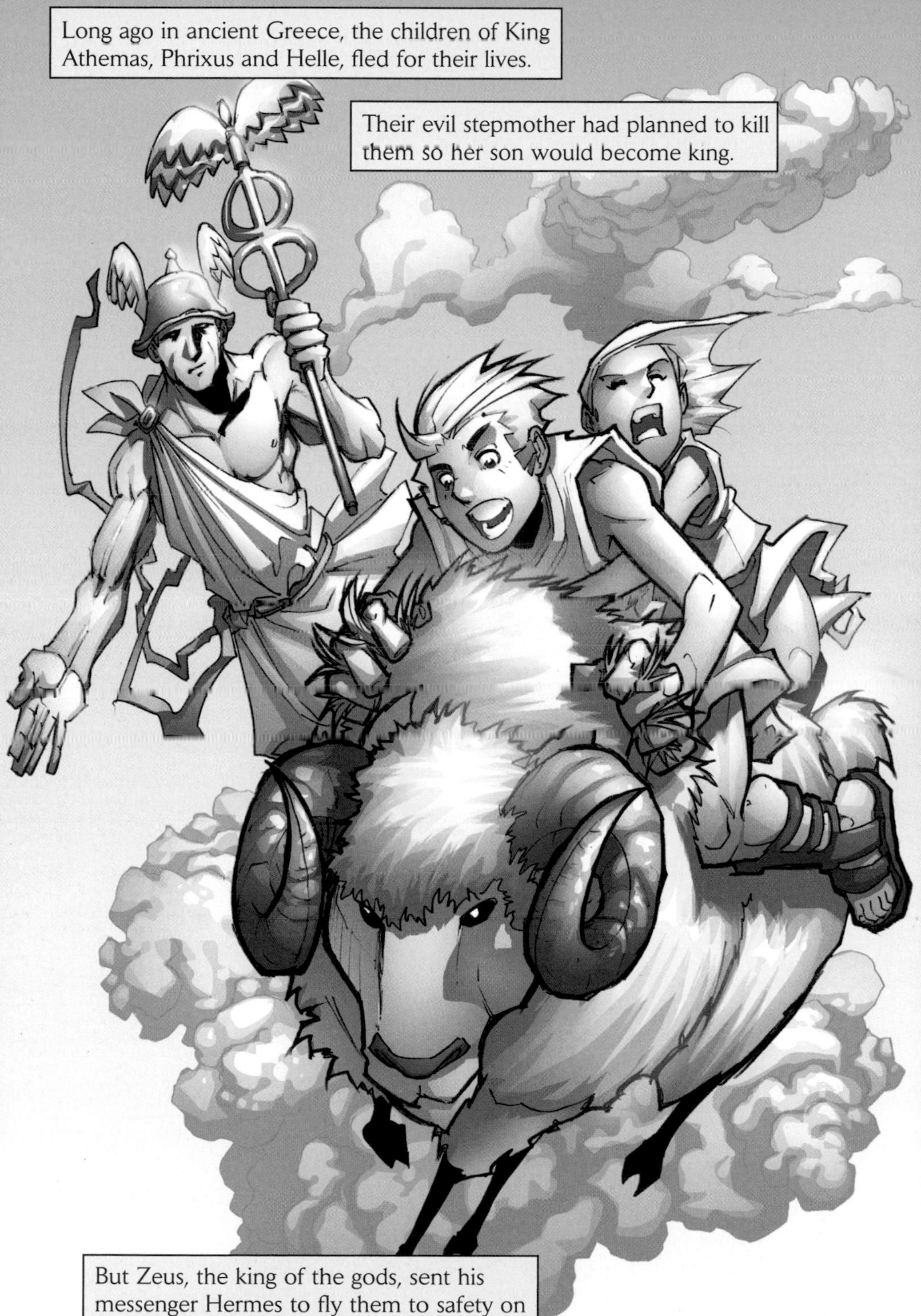
Long ago in ancient Greece, the children of King Athemas, Phrixus and Helle, fled for their lives.
Their evil stepmother had planned to kill them so her son would become king.
But Zeus, the king of the gods, sent his messenger Hermes to fly them to safety on the back of the golden-fleeced ram, Aries.

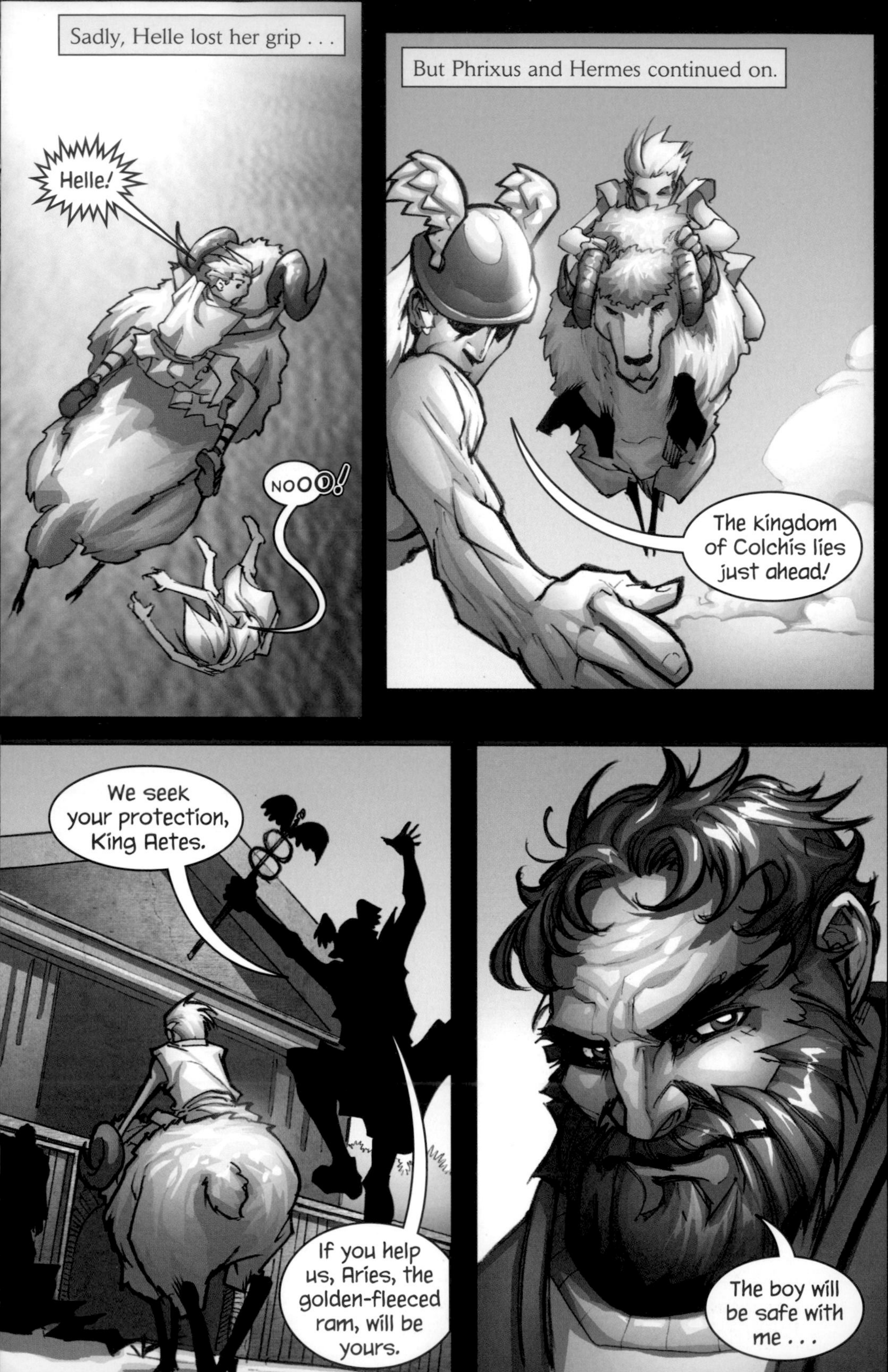
Sadly, Helle lost her grip . . .
Helle!
NOOO!
But Phrixus and Hermes continued on.
The kingdom of Colchis lies just ahead!
We seek your protection, King Aetes.
If you help us, Aries, the golden-fleeced ram, will be yours.
The boy will be safe with me . . .

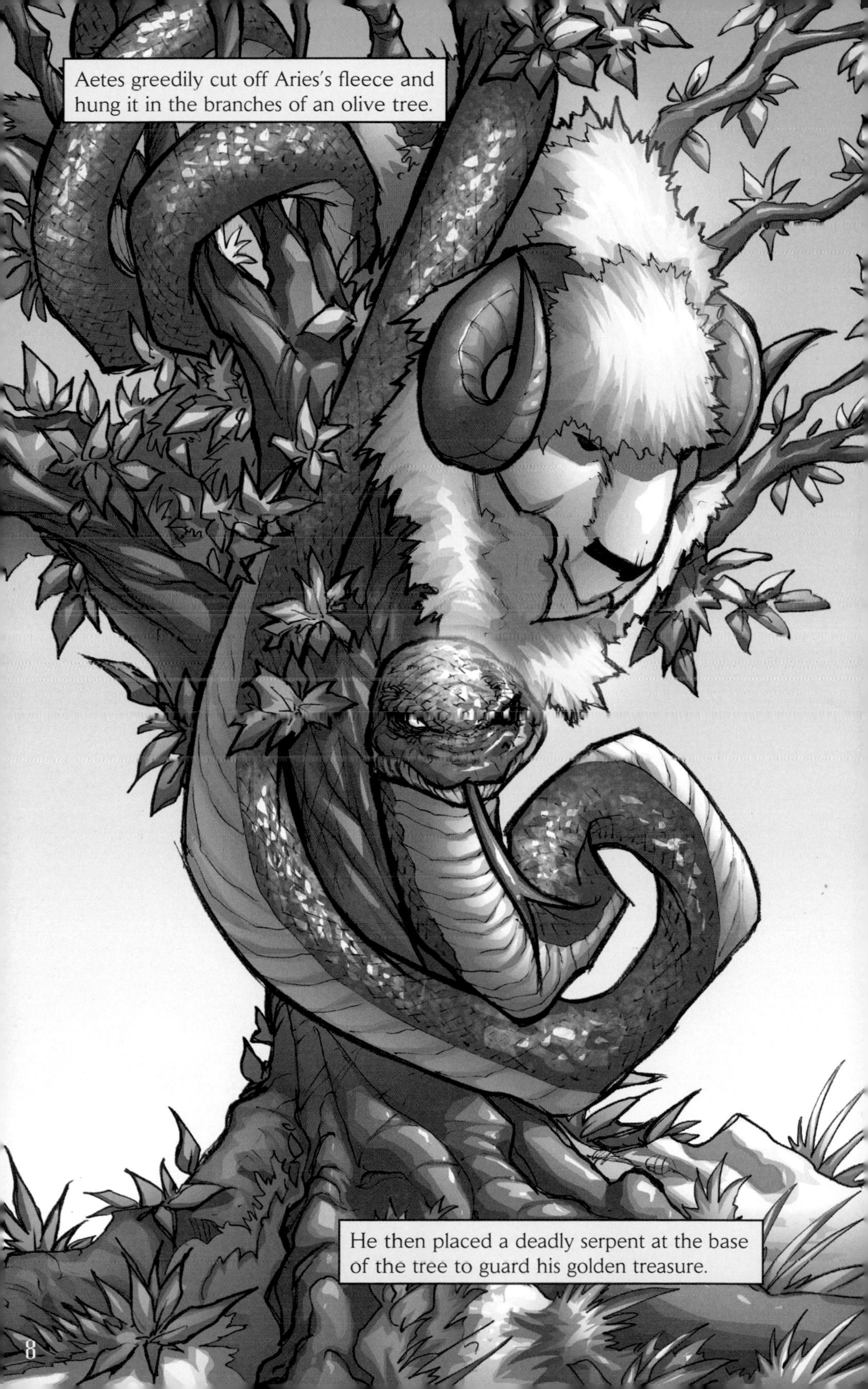
Aetes greedily cut off Aries's fleece and hung it in the branches of an olive tree.
He then placed a deadly serpent at the base of the tree to guard his golden treasure.

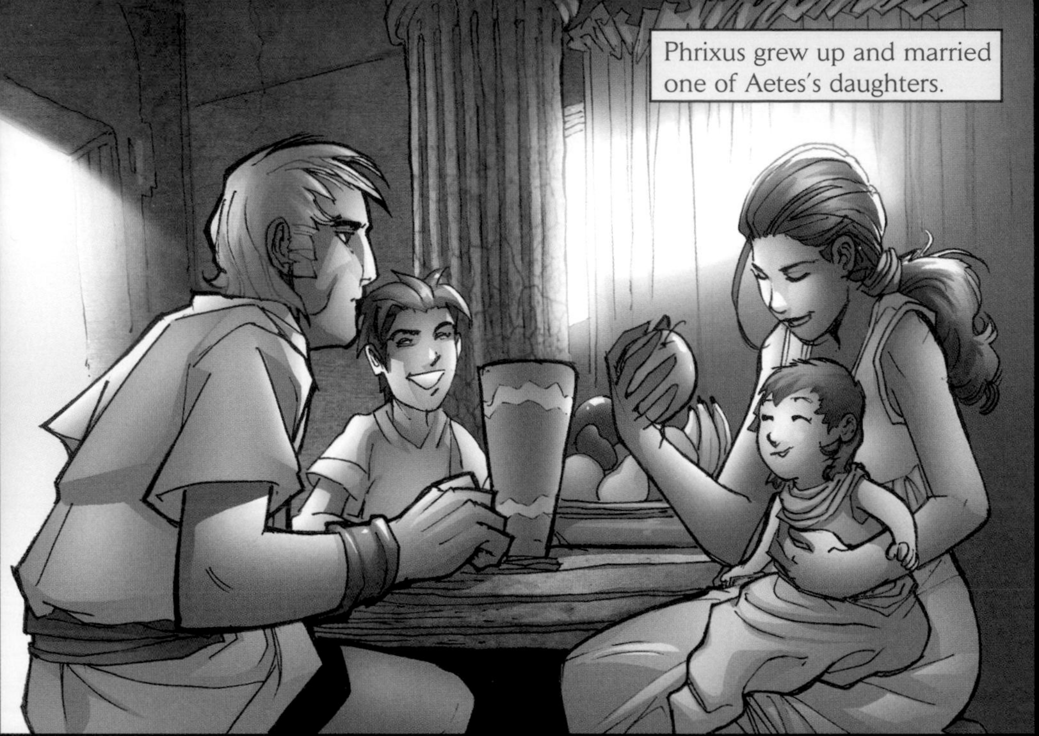
Phrixus grew up and married one of Aetes's daughters.

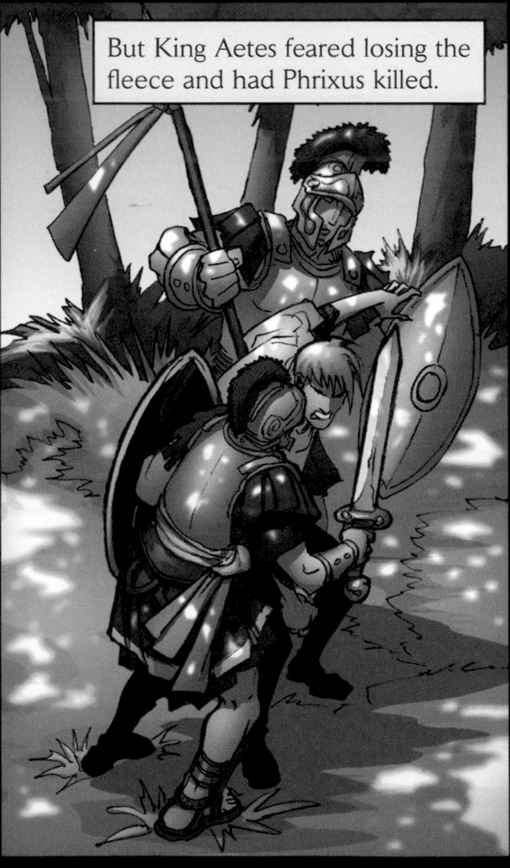
But King Aetes feared losing the fleece and had Phrixus killed.

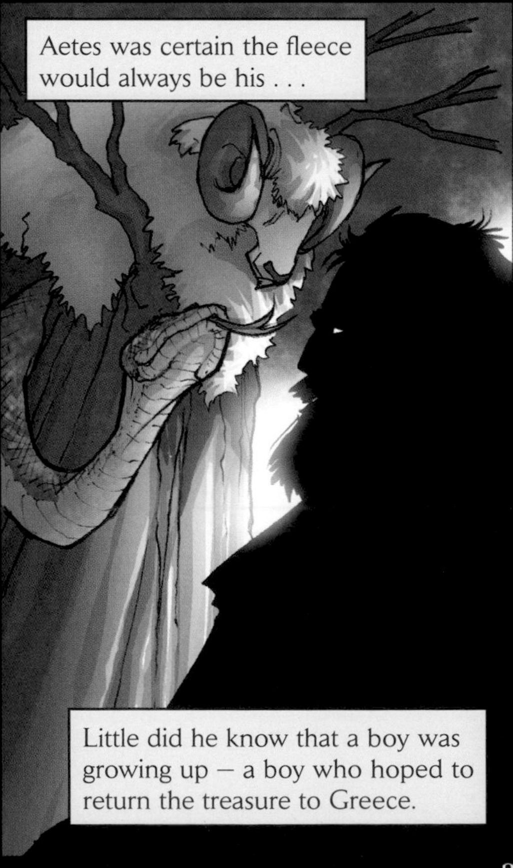
Aetes was certain the fleece would always be his . . .
Little did he know that a boy was growing up – a boy who hoped to return the treasure to Greece.

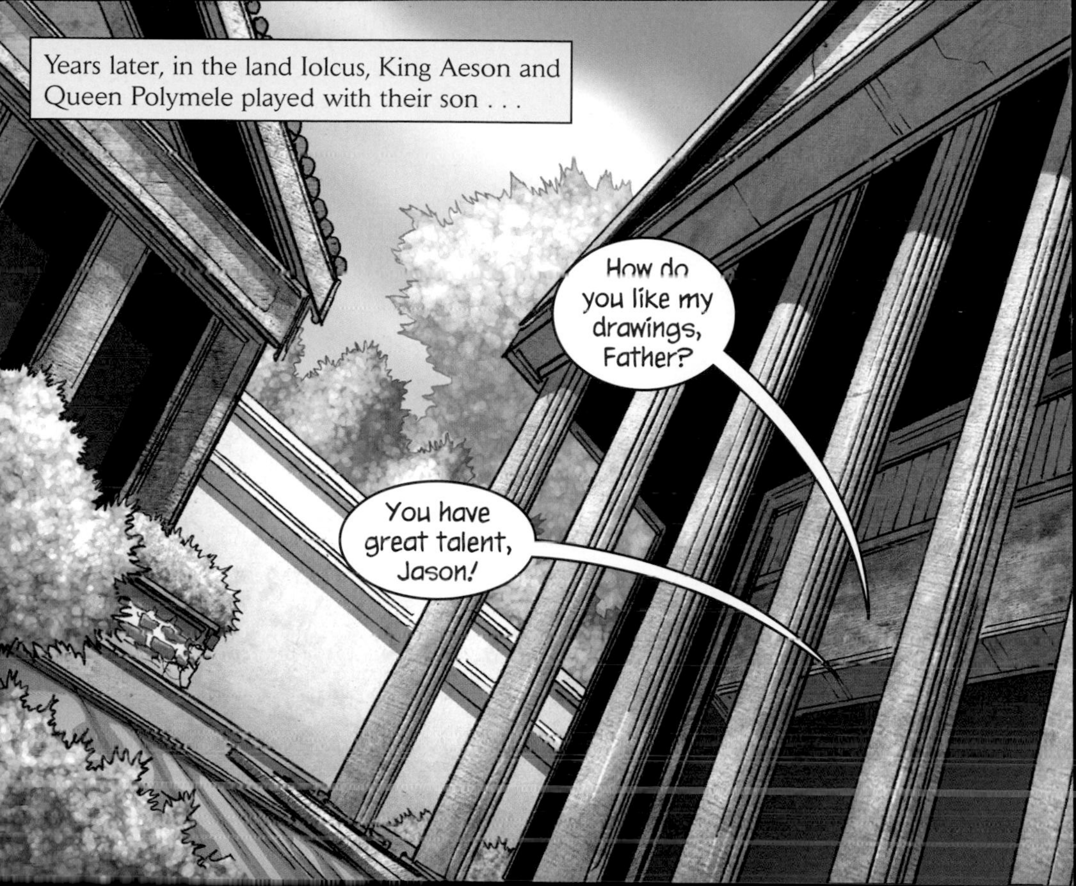
Years later, in the land Iolcus, King Aeson and Queen Polymele played with their son . . .
How do you like my drawings, Father?
You have great talent, Jason!

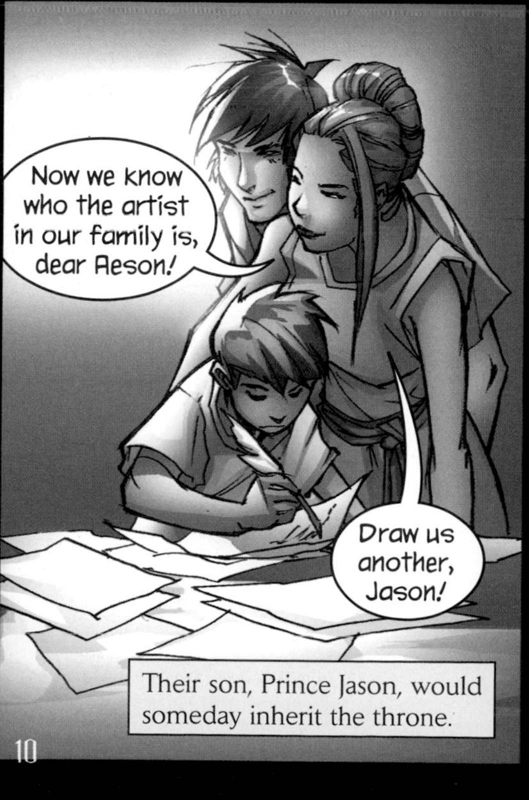
Now we know who the artist in our family is, dear Aeson!
Draw us another, Jason!
Their son, Prince Jason, would someday inherit the throne.

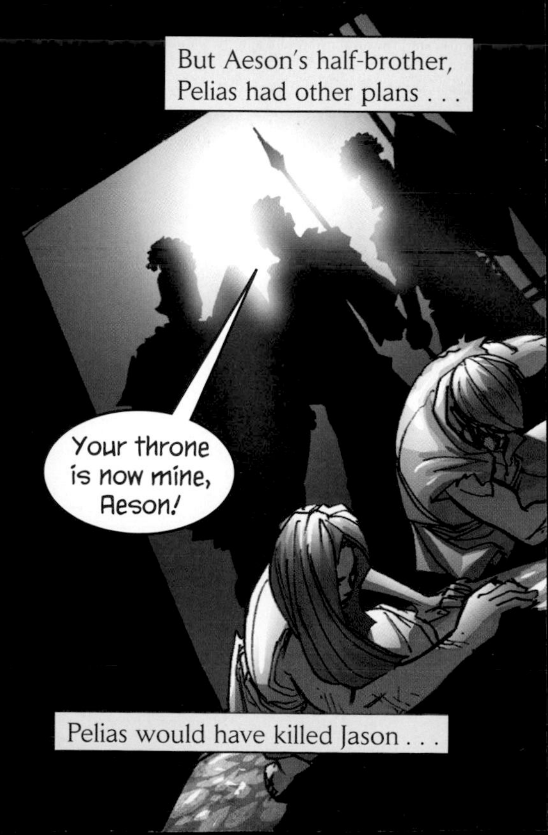
But Aeson's half-brother, Pelias had other plans . . .
Your throne is now mine, Aeson!
Pelias would have killed Jason . . .

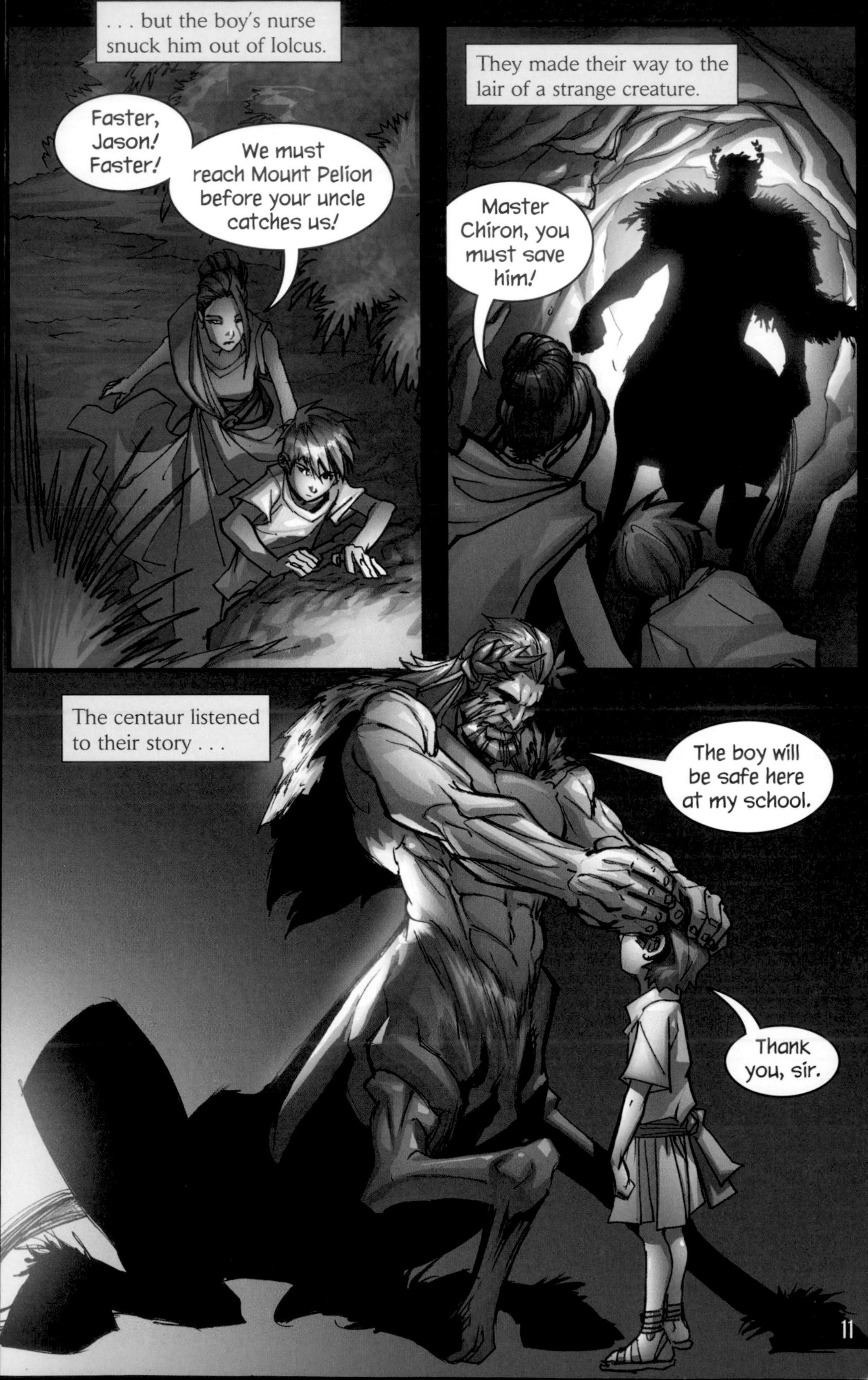
. . . but the boy's nurse snuck him out of Iolcus.
Faster, Jason! Faster!
We must reach Mount Pelion before your uncle catches us!
They made their way to the lair of a strange creature.
Master Chiron, you must save him!
The centaur listened to their story . . .
The boy will be safe here at my school.
Thank you, sir.

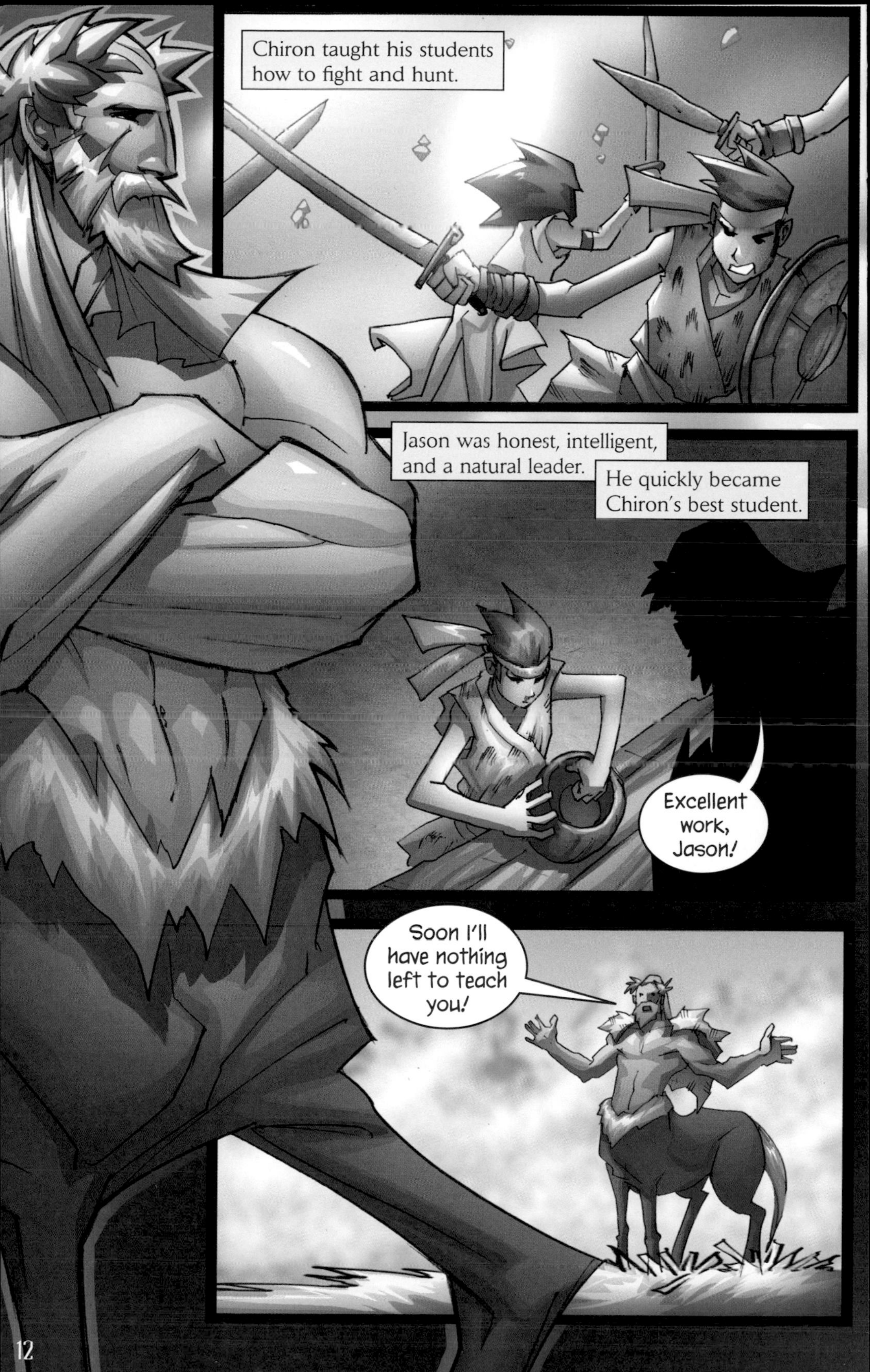
Chiron taught his students how to fight and hunt.
Jason was honest, intelligent, and a natural leader.
He quickly became Chiron's best student.
Excellent work, Jason!
Soon I'll have nothing left to teach you!

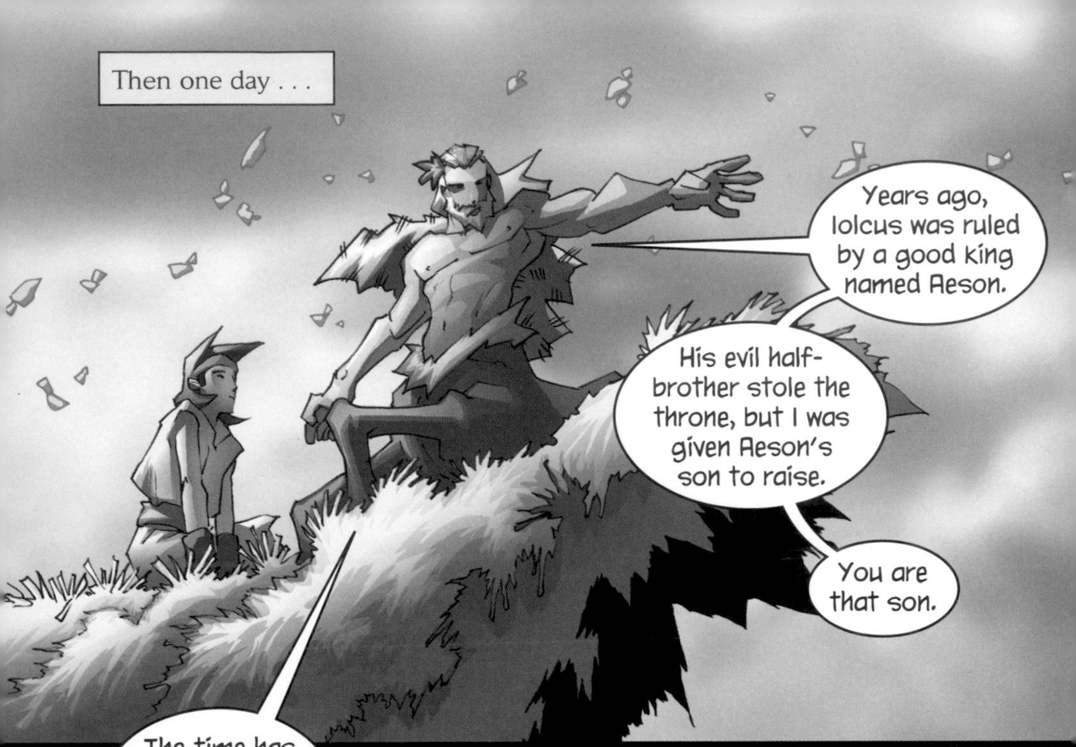
Then one day . . .
Years ago, Iolcus was ruled by a good king named Aeson.
His evil half-brother stole the throne, but I was given Aeson's son to raise.
You are that son.

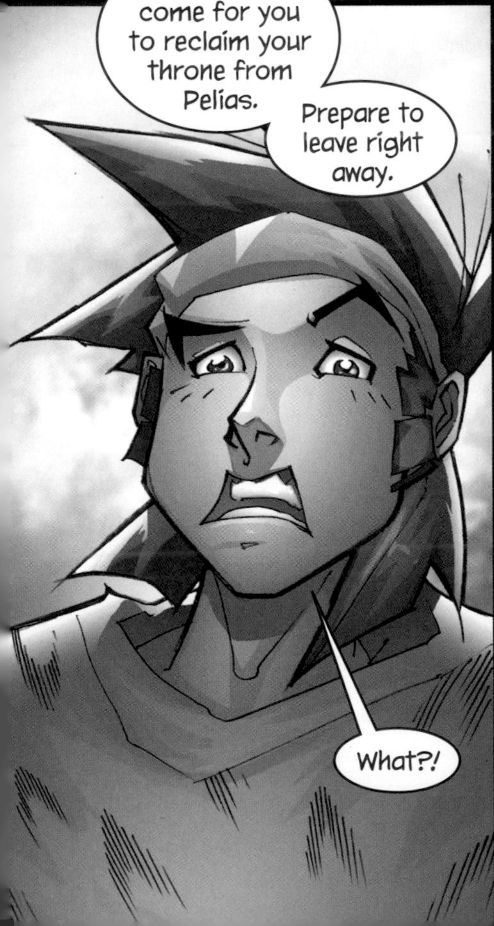
The time has come for you to reclaim your throne from Pelias.
Prepare to leave right away.
What?!

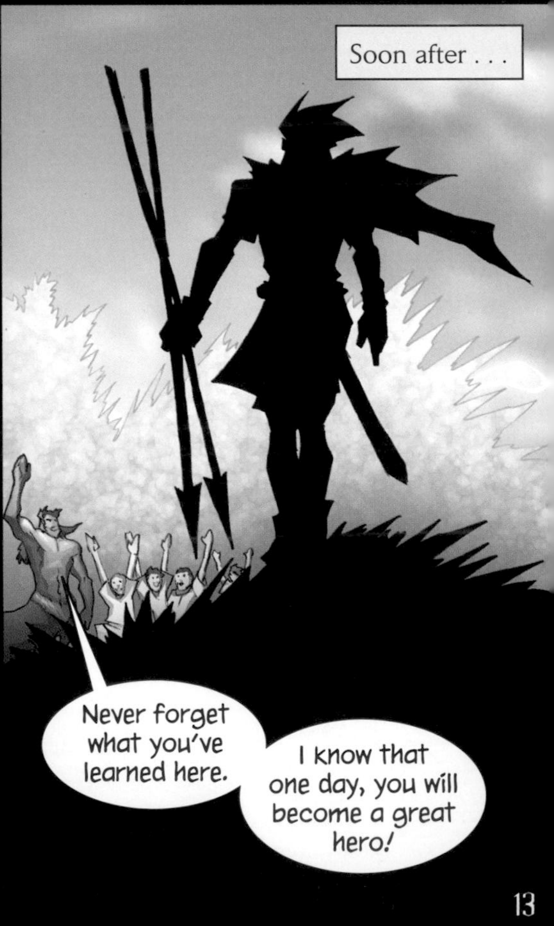
Soon after . . .
Never forget what you've learned here.
I know that one day, you will become a great hero!

CHAPTER 2: THE QUEST BEGINS

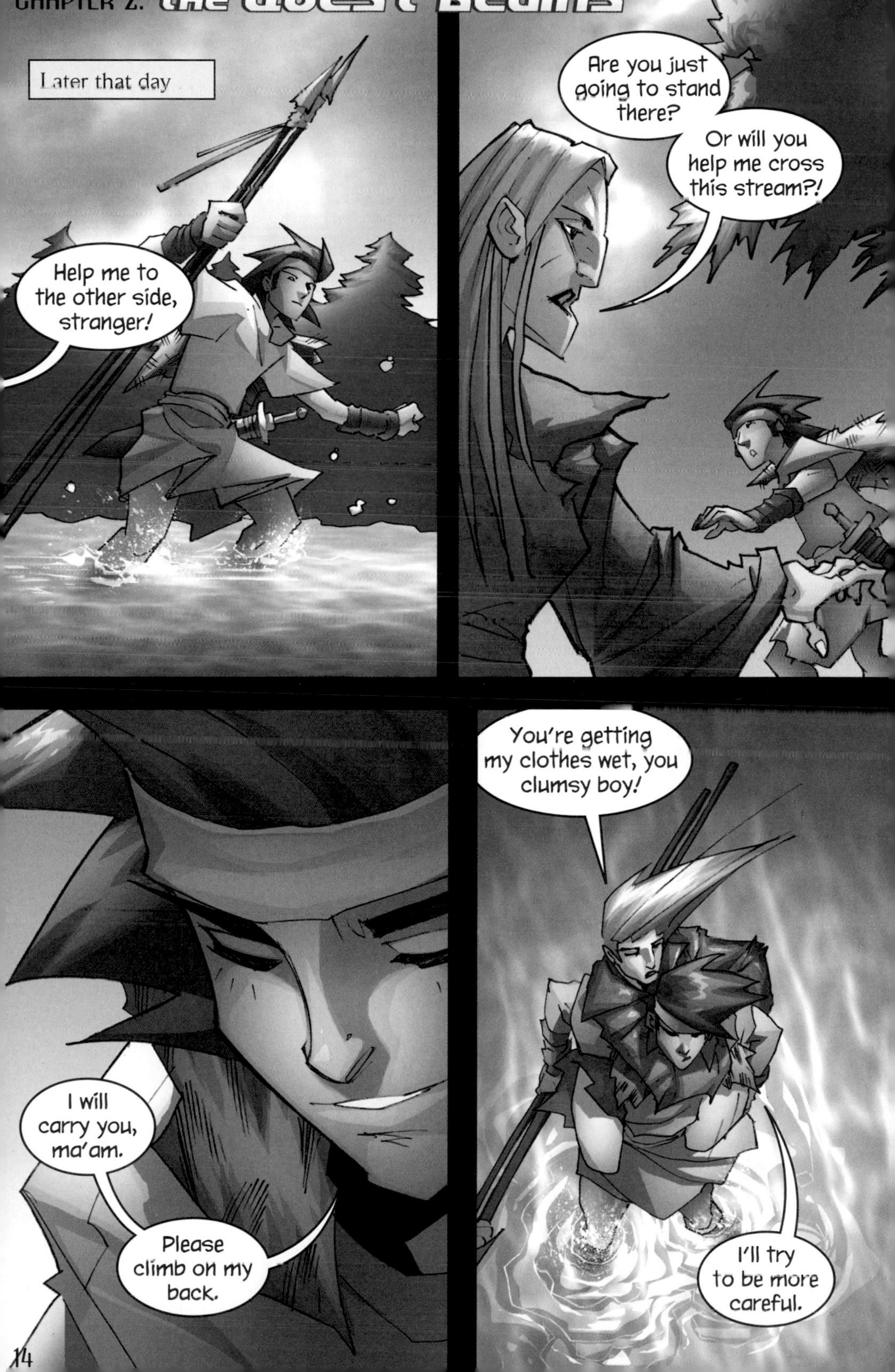
Later that day . . .
Help me to the other side, stranger!
Are you just going to stand there?
Or will you help me cross this stream?!
I will carry you, ma'am.
Please climb on my back.
You're getting my clothes wet, you clumsy boy!
I'll try to be more careful.

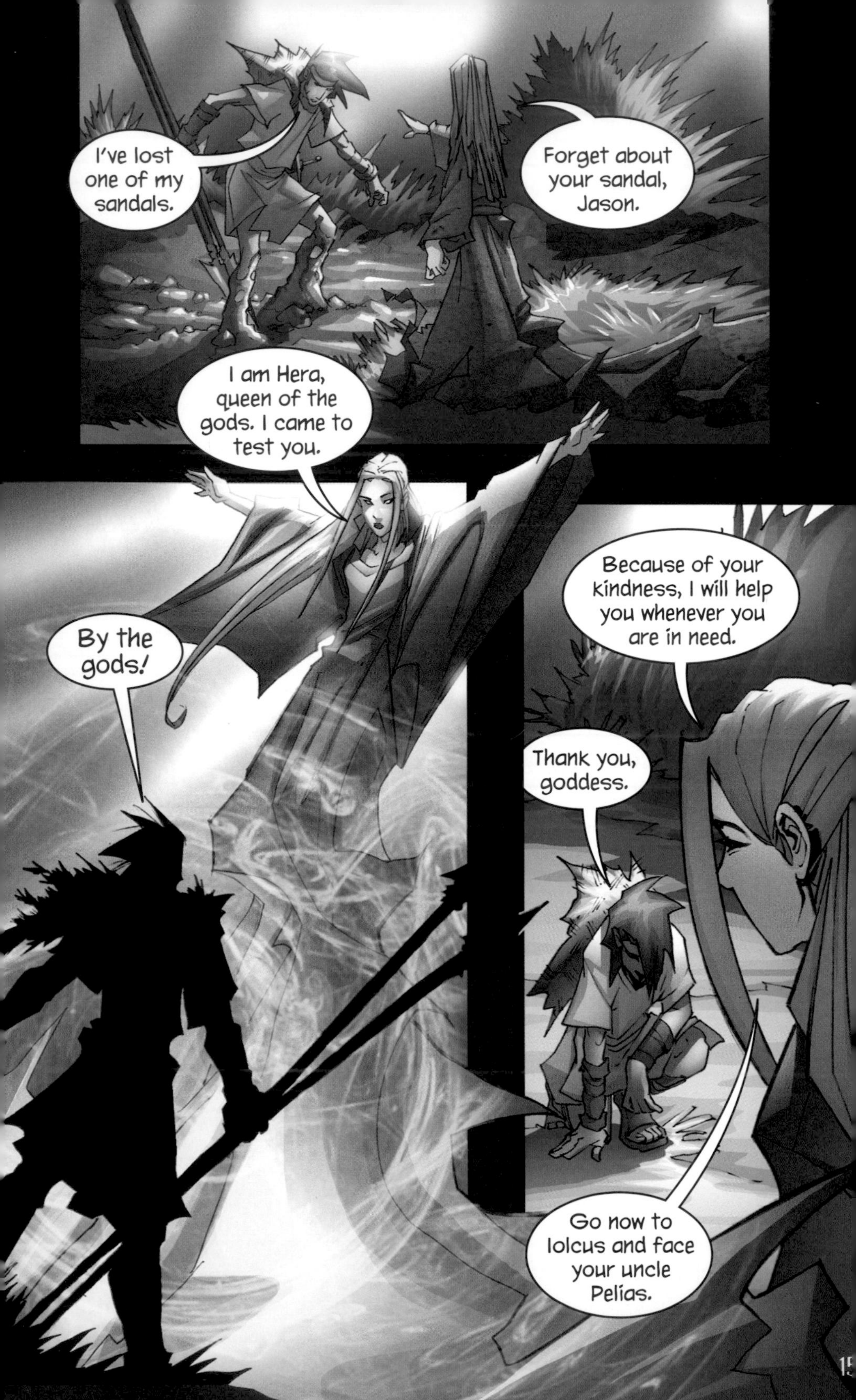
I've lost one of my sandals.
Forget about your sandal, Jason.
I am Hera, queen of the gods. I came to test you.
By the gods!
Because of your kindness, I will help you whenever you are in need.
Thank you, goddess.
Go now to Iolcus and face your uncle Pelias.

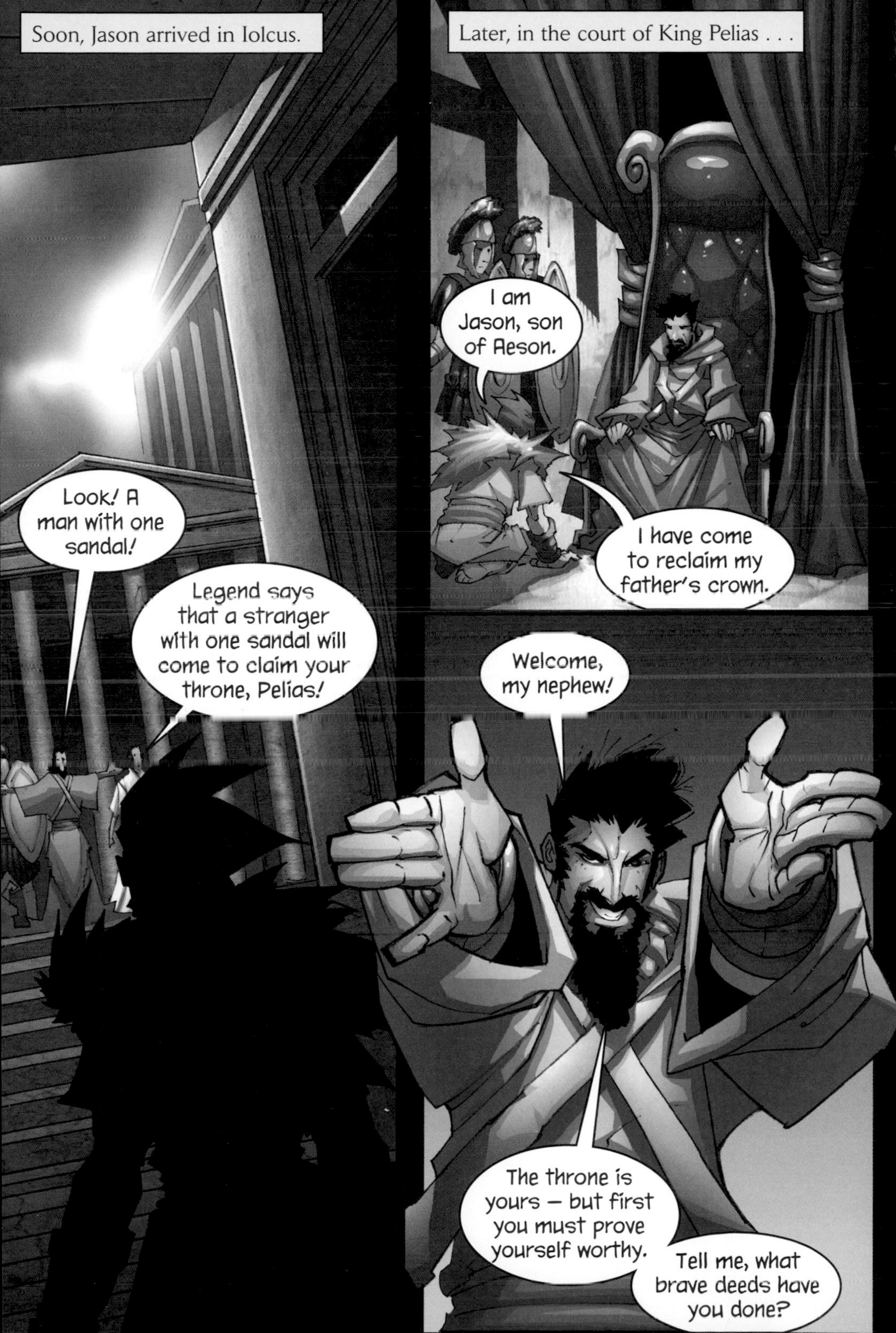
Soon, Jason arrived in Iolcus.
Look! A man with one sandal!
Legend says that a stranger with one sandal will come to claim your throne, Pelias!
Later, in the court of King Pelias . . .
I am Jason, son of Aeson.
I have come to reclaim my father's crown.
Welcome, my nephew!
The throne is yours — but first you must prove yourself worthy.
Tell me, what brave deeds have you done?

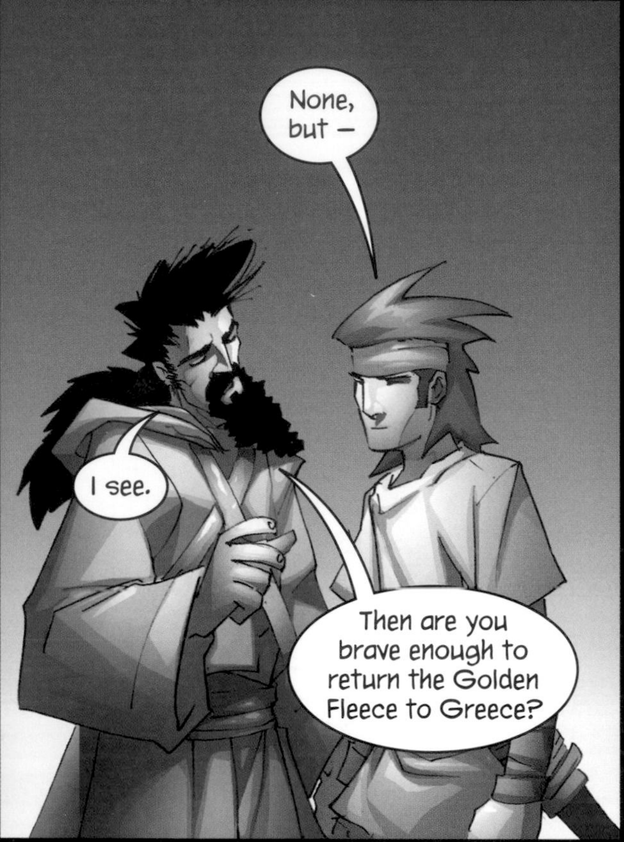
None, but –
I see.
Then are you brave enough to return the Golden Fleece to Greece?
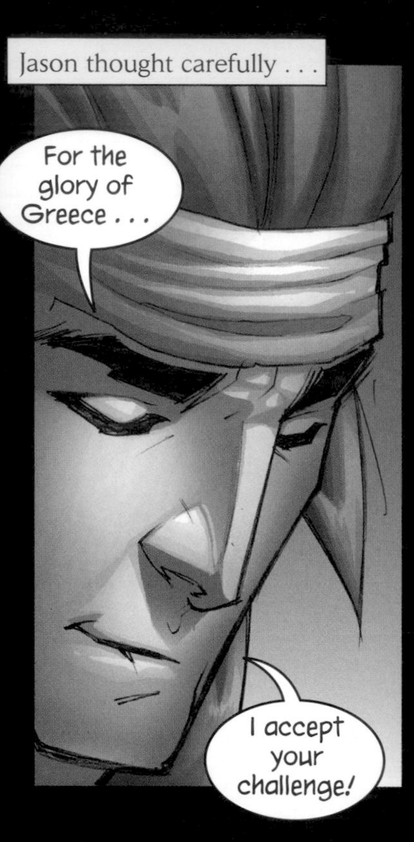
Jason thought carefully . . .
For the glory of Greece . . .
I accept your challenge!
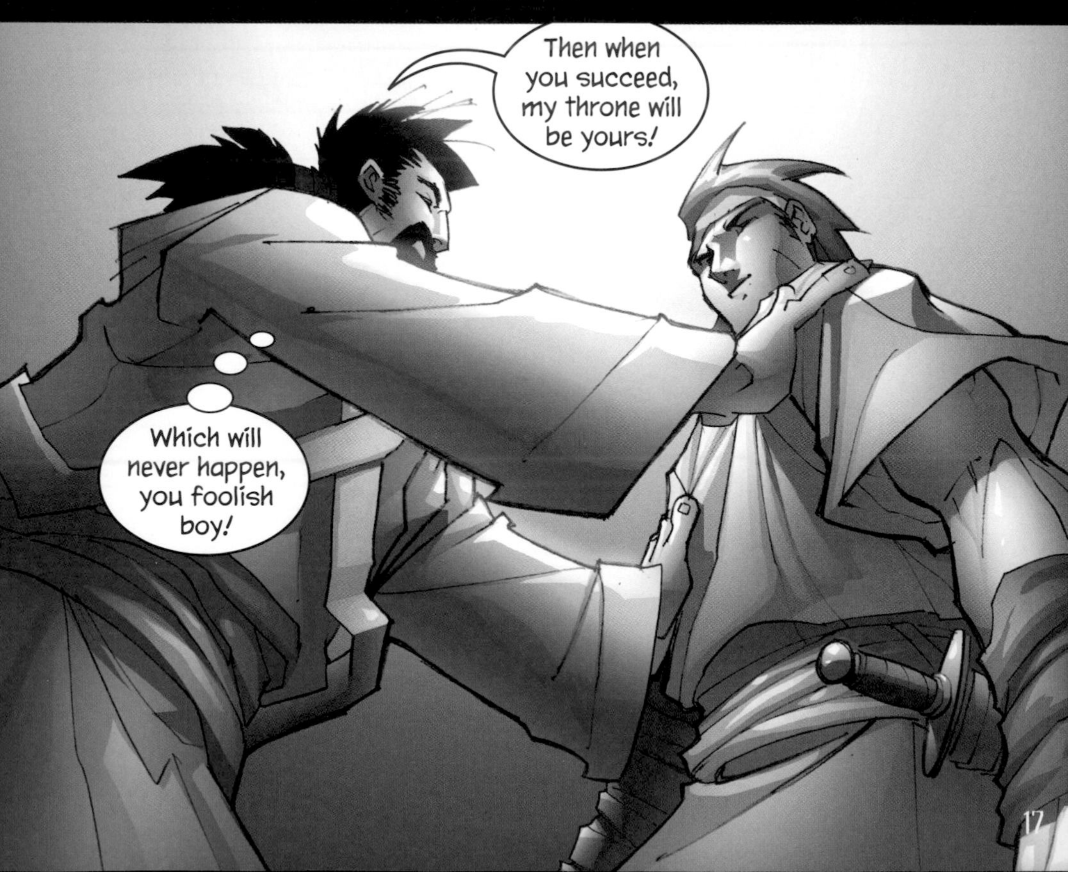
Then when you succeed, my throne will be yours!
Which will never happen, you foolish boy!

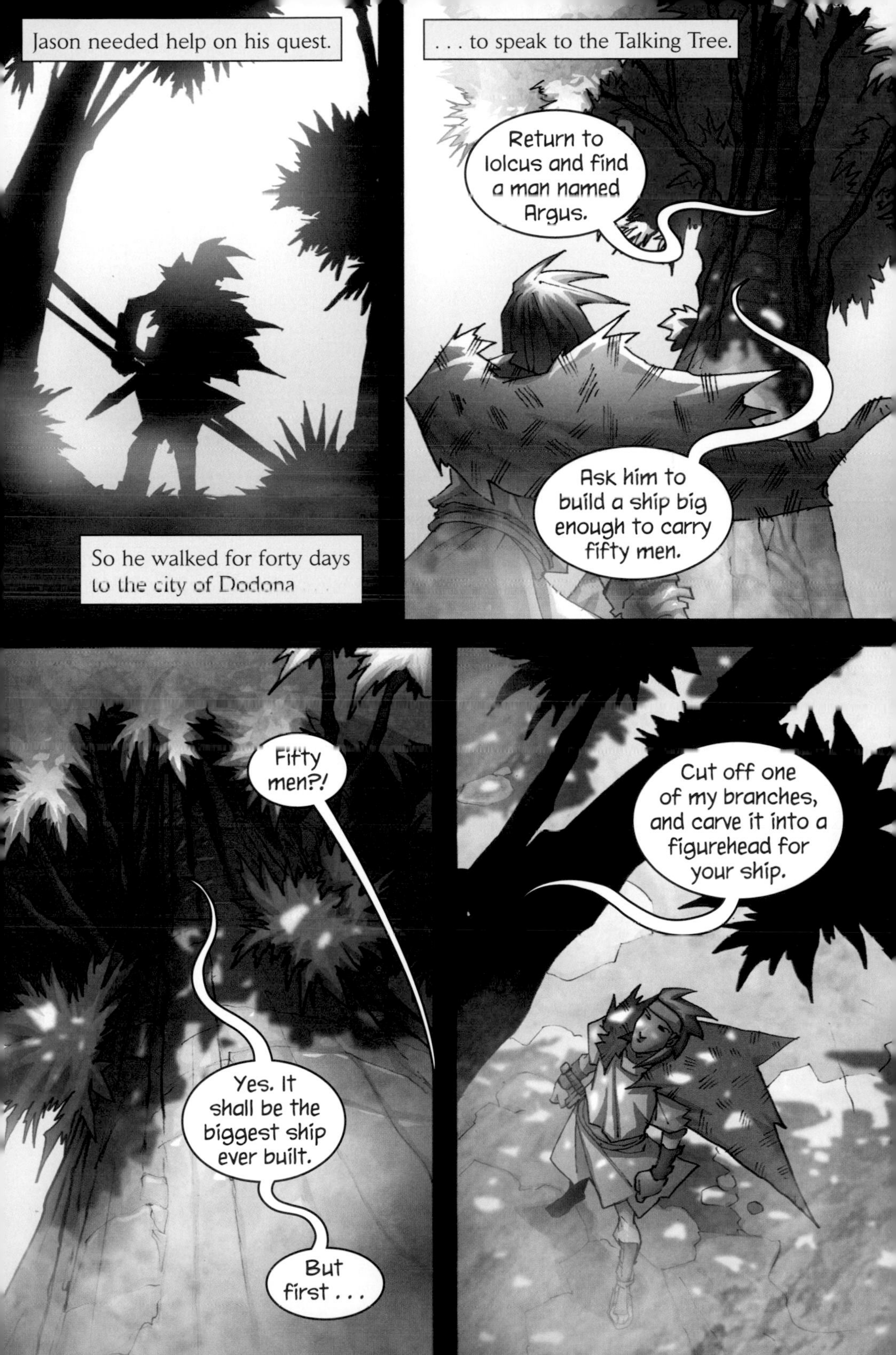

Jason needed help on his quest.
So he walked for forty days to the city of Dodona . . .
. . . to speak to the Talking Tree.
Return to Iolcus and find a man named Argus.
Ask him to build a ship big enough to carry fifty men.
Fifty men?!
Yes. It shall be the biggest ship ever built.
But first . . .
Cut off one of my branches, and carve it into a figurehead for your ship.

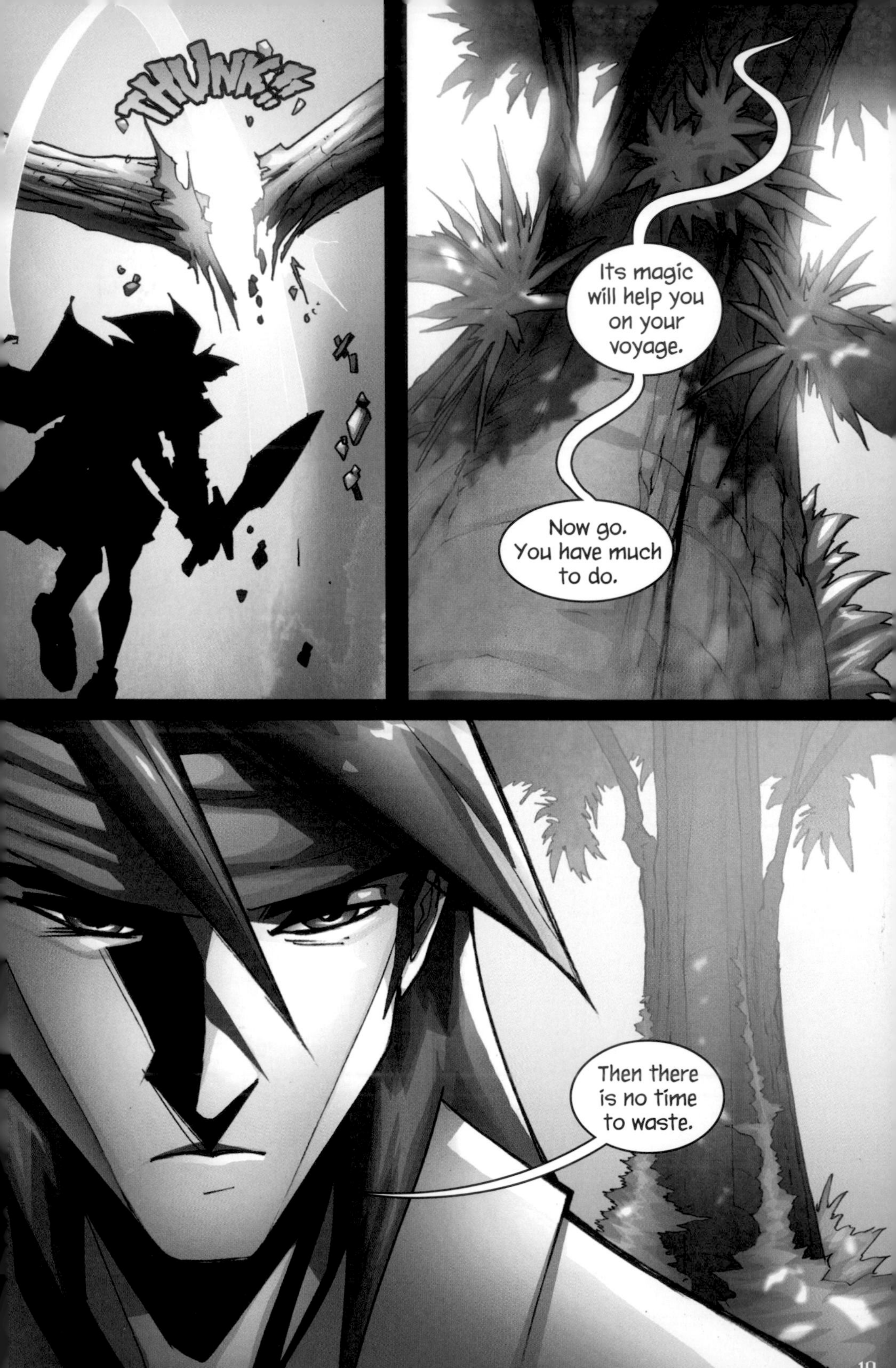
THUNK!!
Its magic will help you on your voyage.
Now go. You have much to do.
Then there is no time to waste.

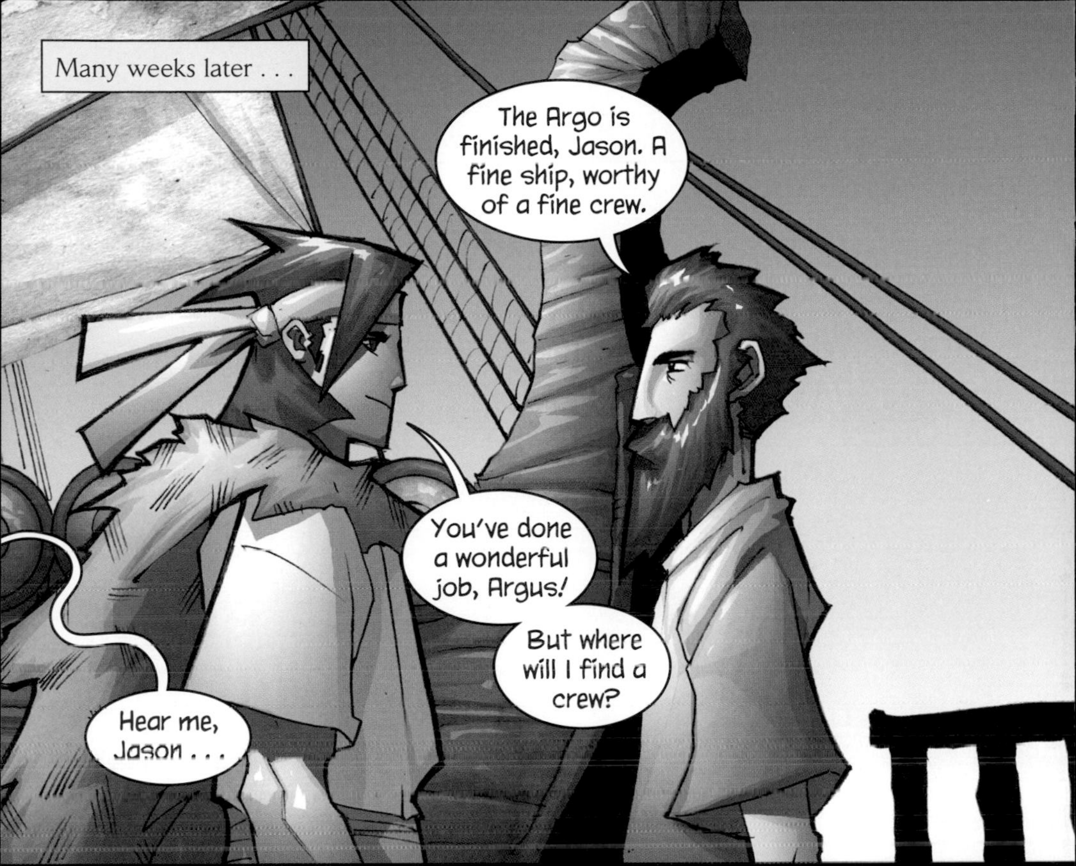
Many weeks later . . .
The Argo is finished, Jason. A fine ship, worthy of a fine crew.
You've done a wonderful job, Argus!
But where will I find a crew?
Hear me, Jason . . .

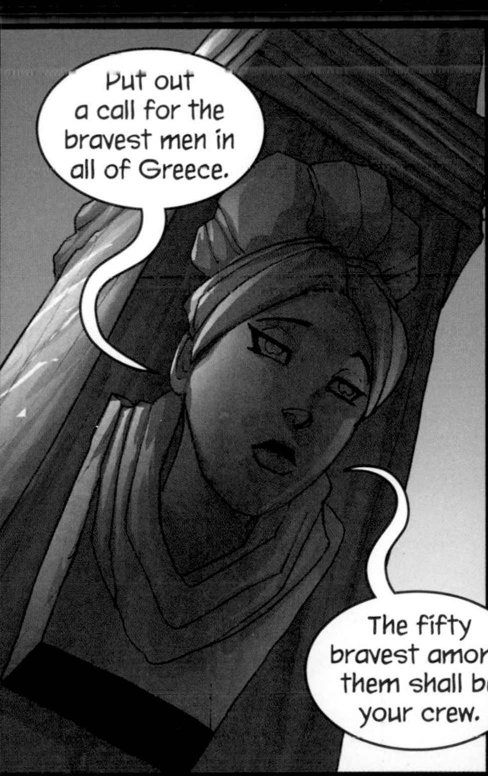
Put out a call for the bravest men in all of Greece.
The fifty bravest among them shall be your crew.

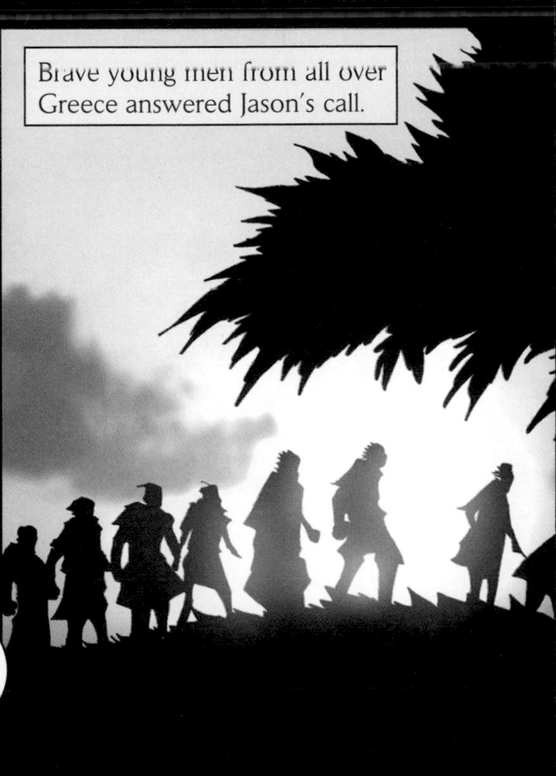
Brave young men from all over Greece answered Jason's call.

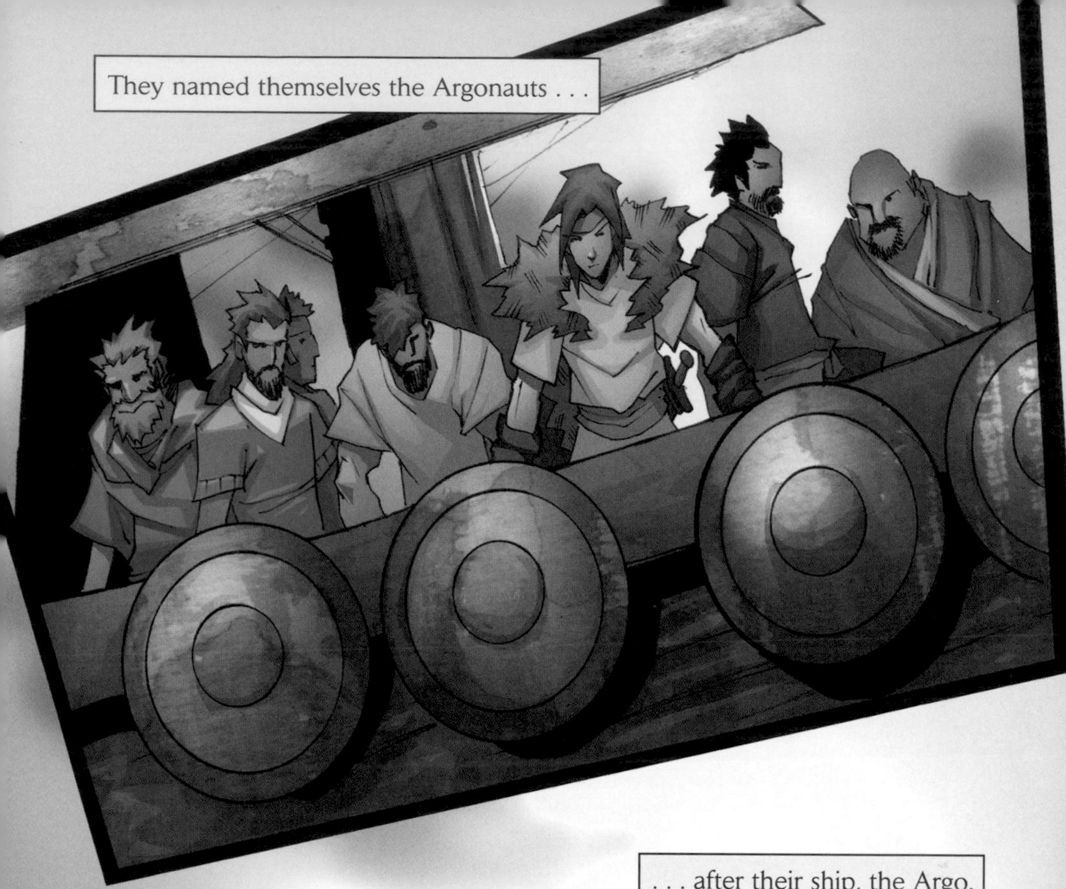
They named themselves the Argonauts . . .

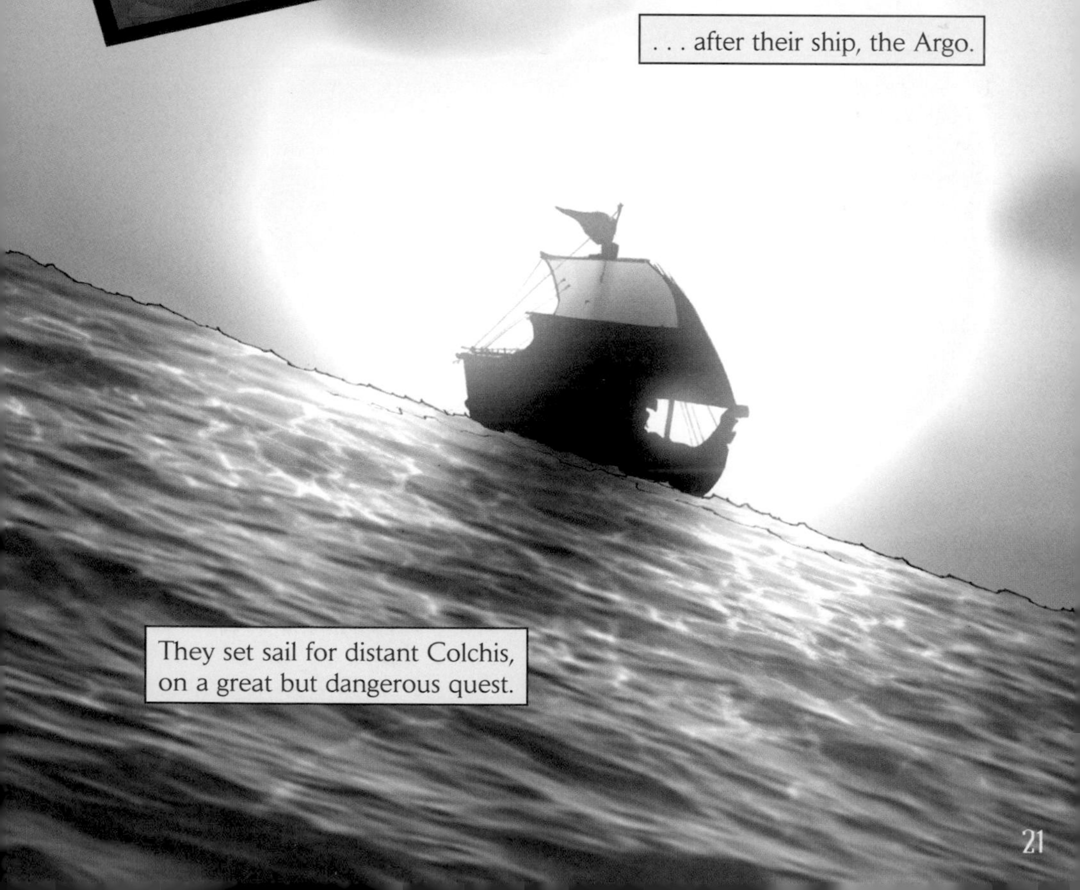
. . . after their ship, the Argo.
They set sail for distant Colchis, on a great but dangerous quest.

CHAPTER 3: DEADLY DEEDS

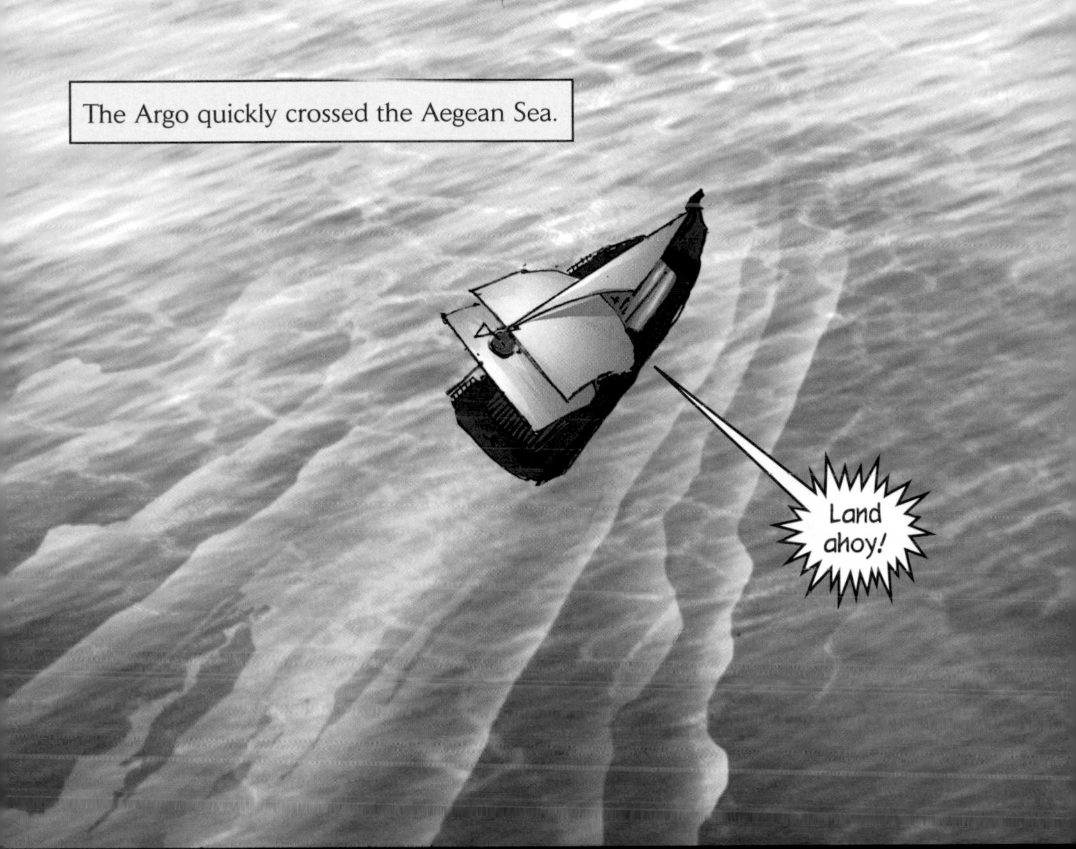
The Argo quickly crossed the Aegean Sea.
Land ahoy!

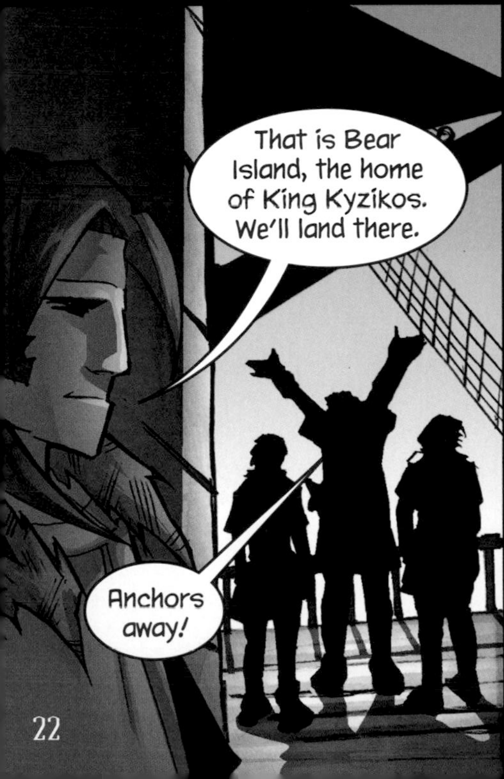
That is Bear Island, the home of King Kyzikos. We'll land there.
Anchors away!

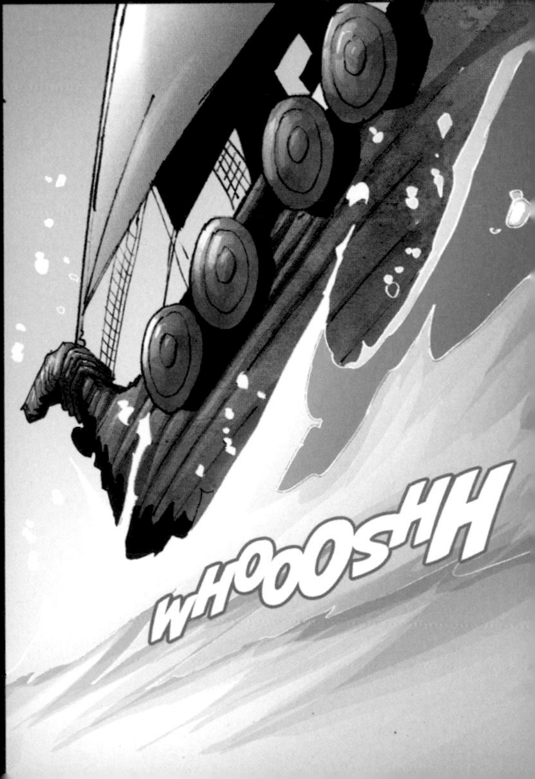
WHOOOSHH

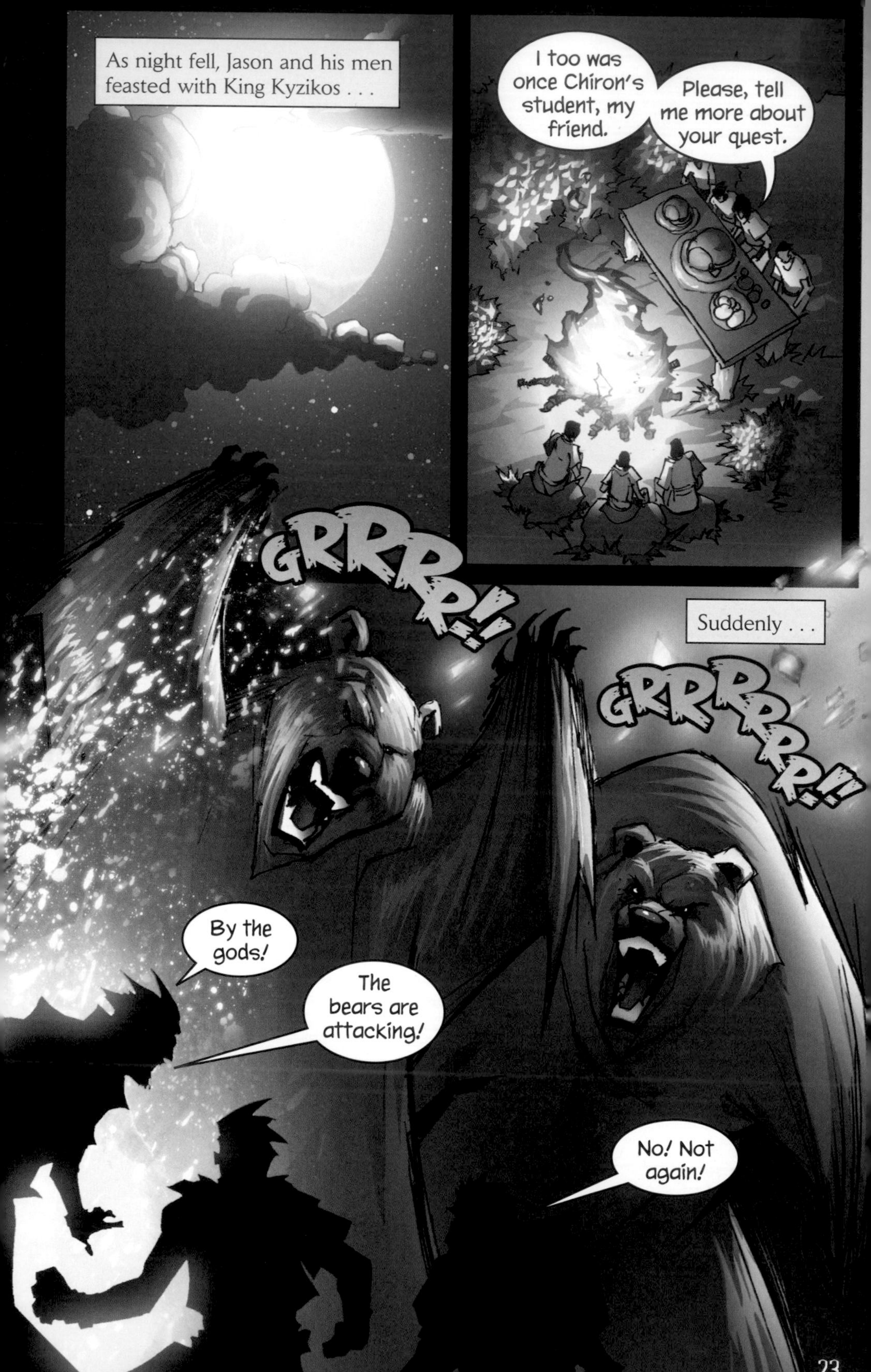
As night fell, Jason and his men feasted with King Kyzikos . . .
I too was once Chiron's student, my friend.
Please, tell me more about your quest.
GRRRR!!
Suddenly . . .
GRRRRRR!!
By the gods!
The bears are attacking!
No! Not again!

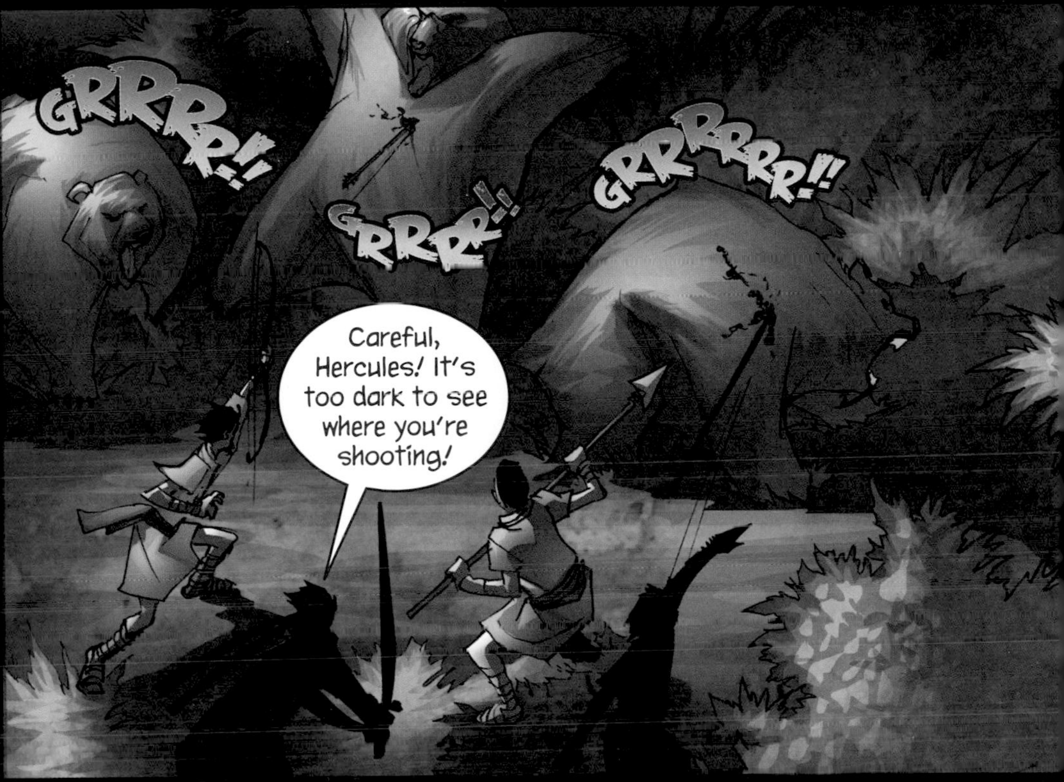
GRRRR!!
GRRRR!!
GRRRRRR!!
Careful, Hercules! It's too dark to see where you're shooting!
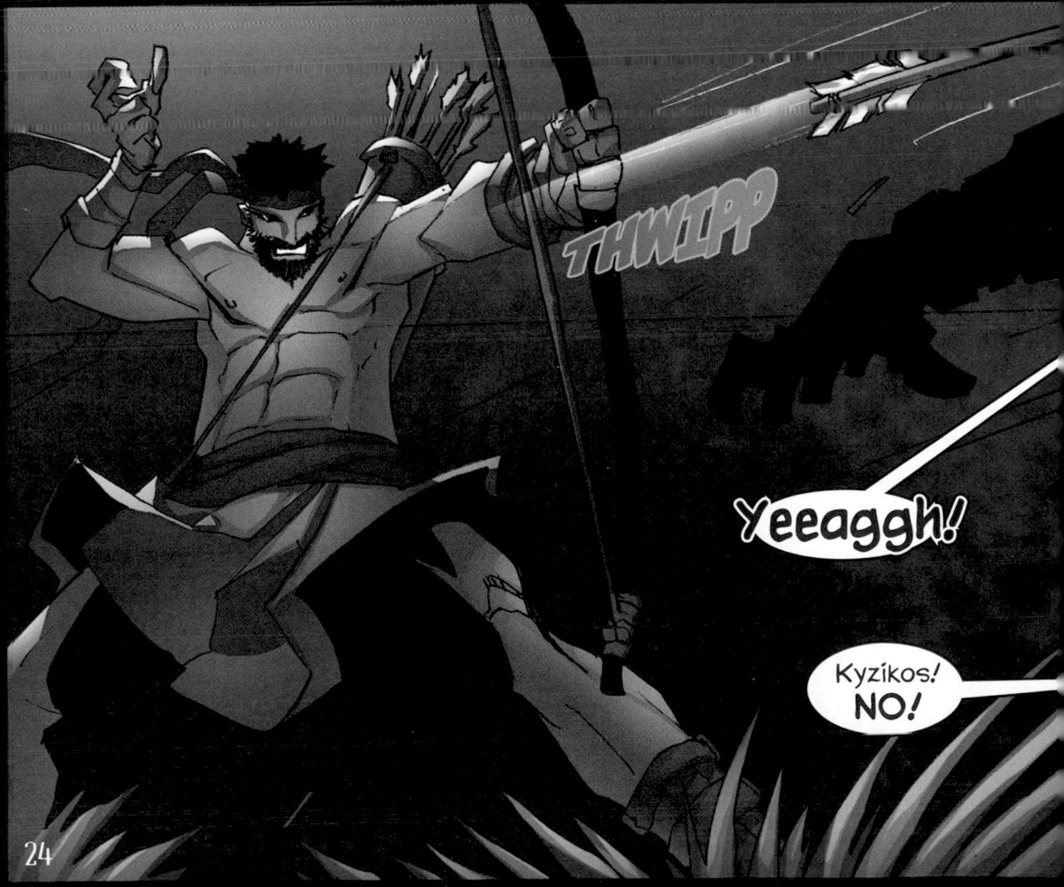
THWIPP
Yeeaggh!
Kyzikos! NO!

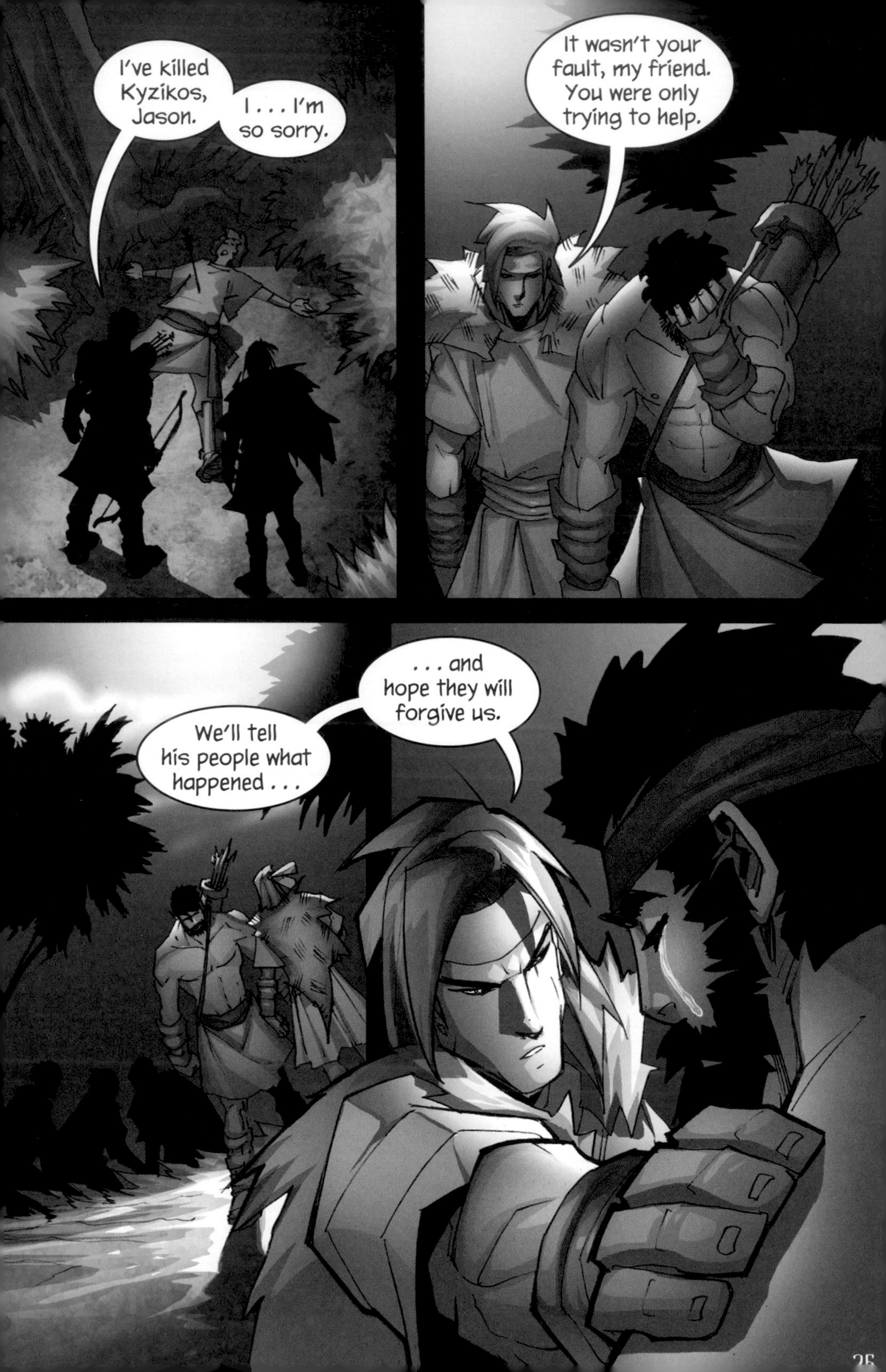
I've killed Kyzikos, Jason.
I . . . I'm so sorry.
It wasn't your fault, my friend. You were only trying to help.
We'll tell his people what happened . . .
. . . and hope they will forgive us.

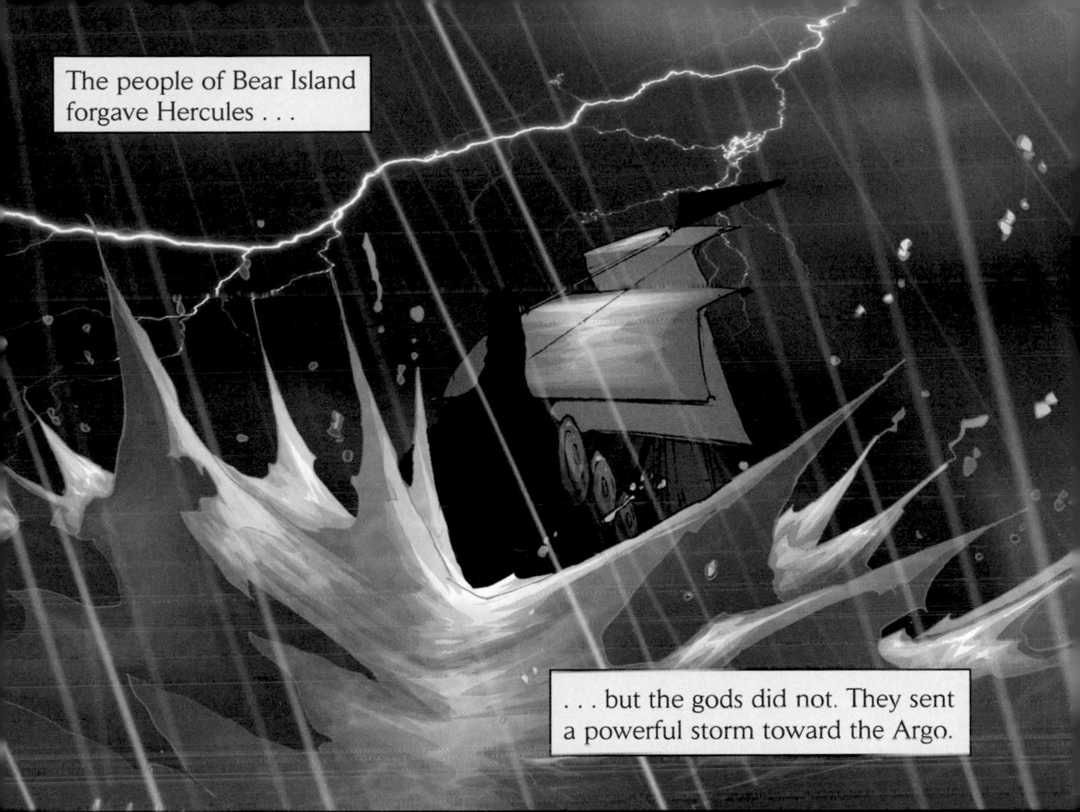
The people of Bear Island forgave Hercules . . .
. . . but the gods did not. They sent a powerful storm toward the Argo.

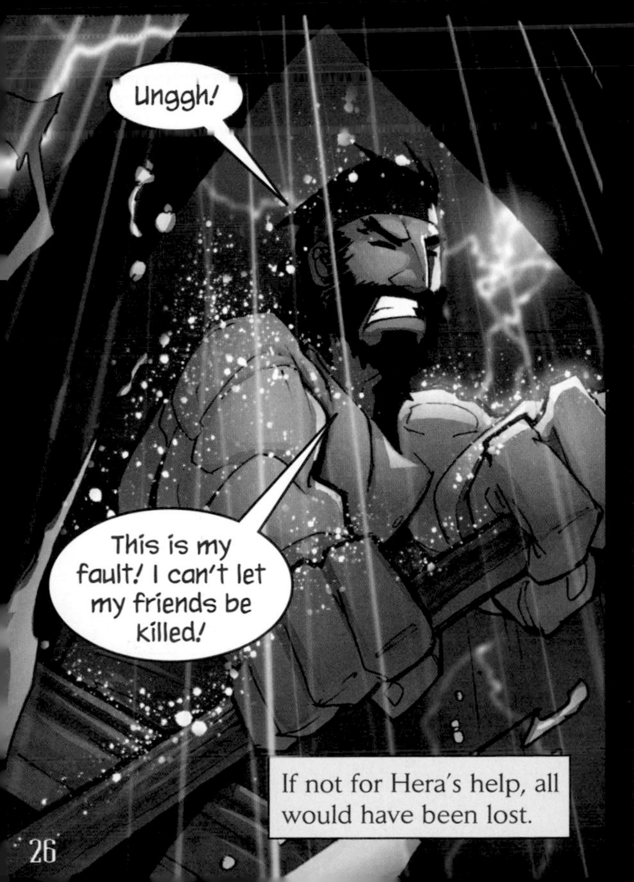
Unggh!
This is my fault! I can't let my friends be killed!
If not for Hera's help, all would have been lost.

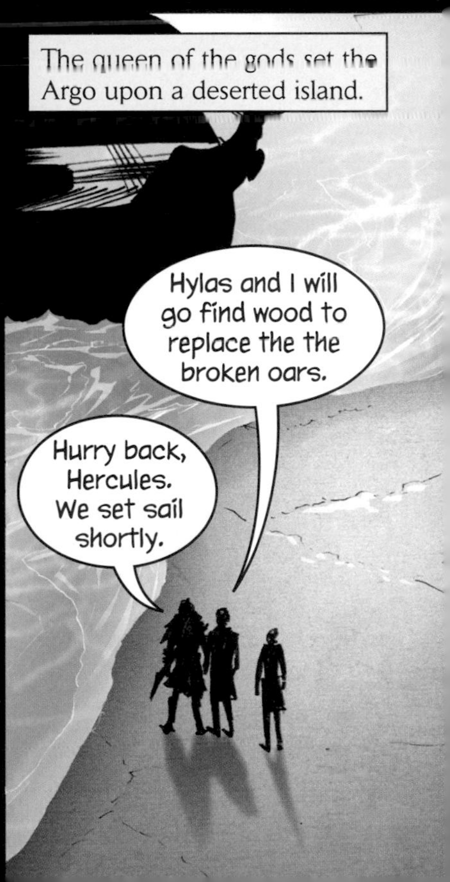
The queen of the gods set the Argo upon a deserted island.
Hylas and I will go find wood to replace the the broken oars.
Hurry back, Hercules. We set sail shortly.

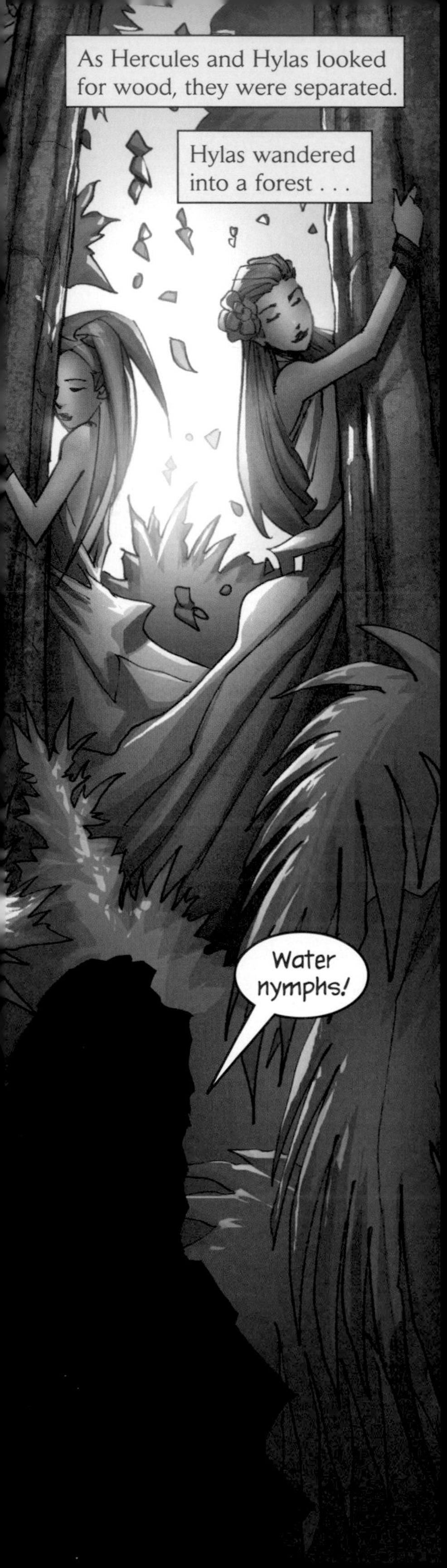
As Hercules and Hylas looked for wood, they were separated.
Hylas wandered into a forest . . .
Water nymphs!

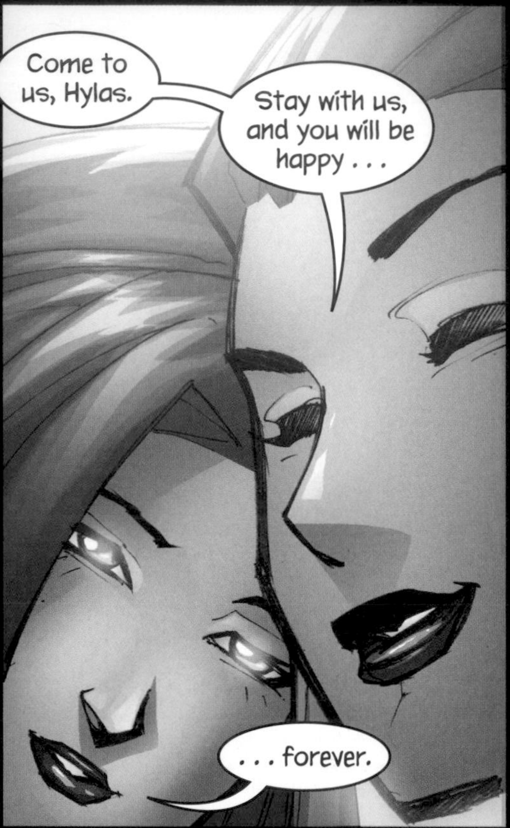
Come to us, Hylas.
Stay with us, and you will be happy . . .
. . . forever.

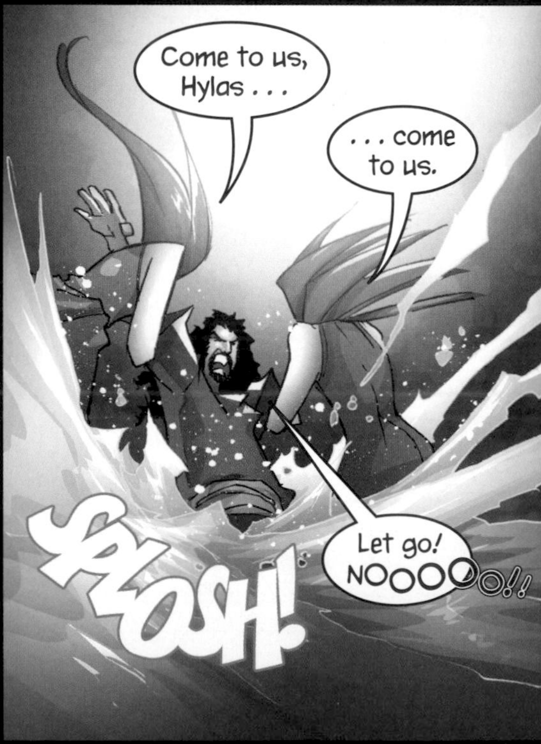
Come to us, Hylas . . .
. . . come to us.
SPLOOSH!
Let go! NOOOOOO!!

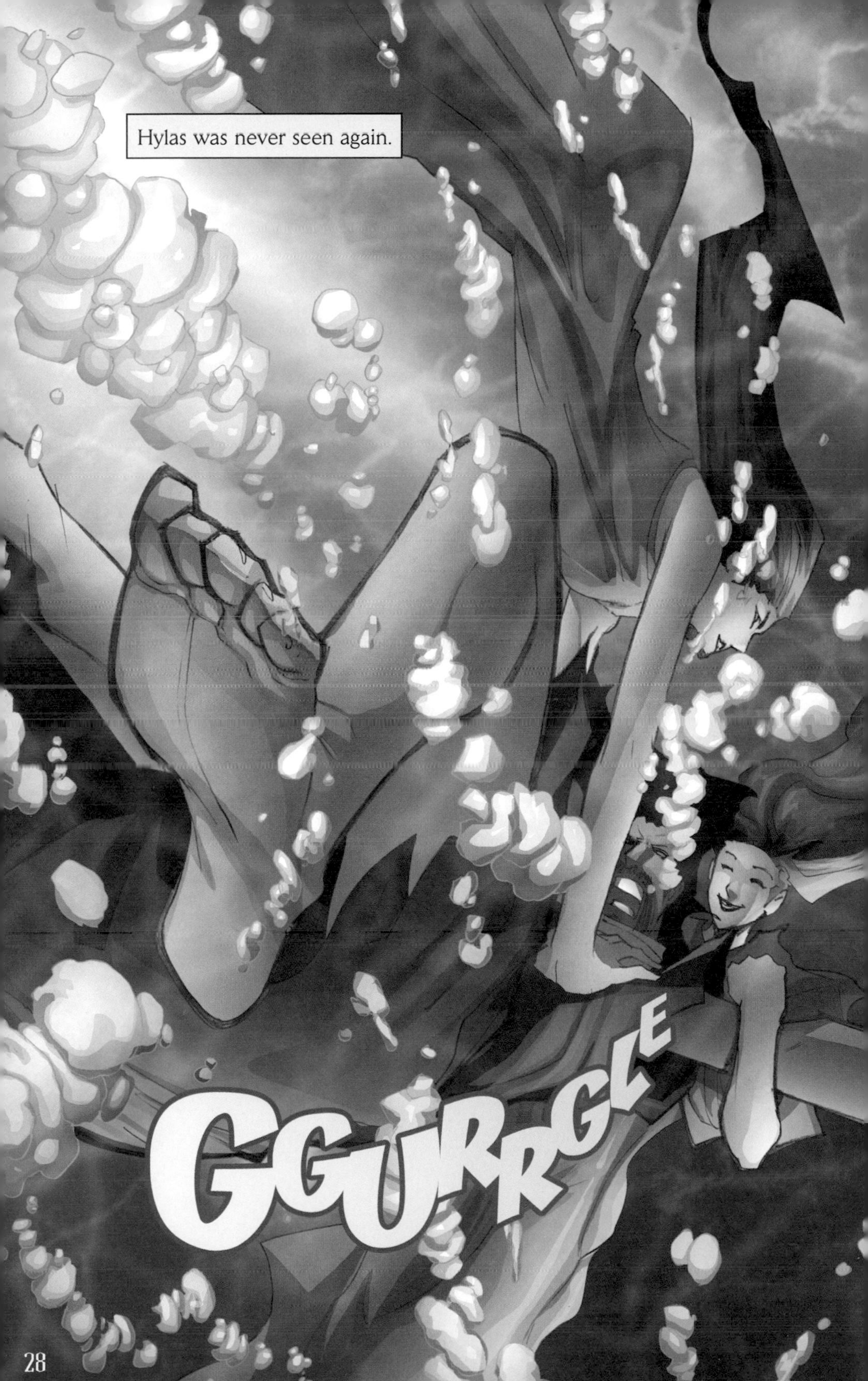
Hylas was never seen again.
GGURRGLE

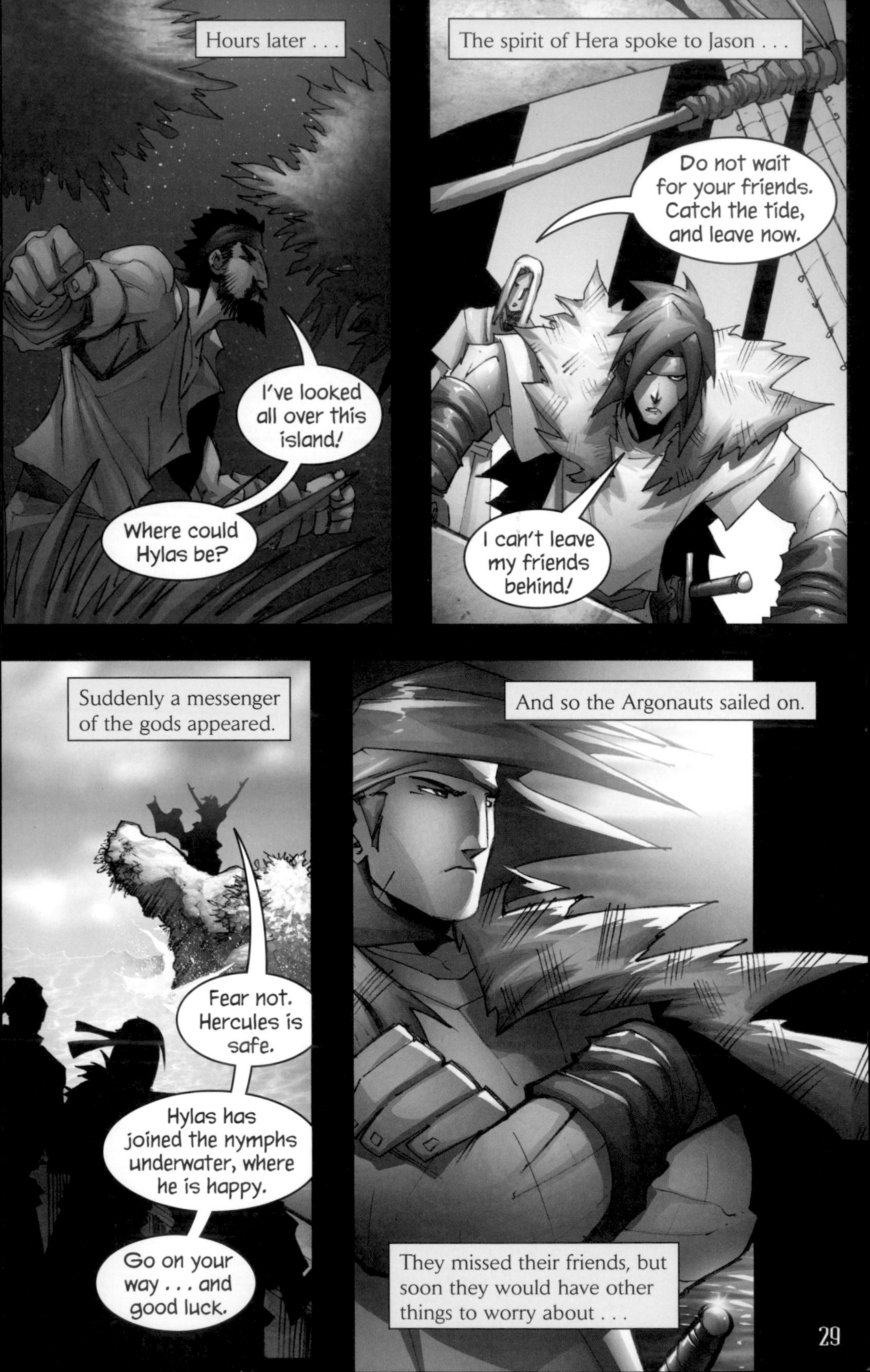

Hours later . . .
I've looked all over this island!
Where could Hylas be?
The spirit of Hera spoke to Jason . . .
Do not wait for your friends. Catch the tide, and leave now.
I can't leave my friends behind!
Suddenly a messenger of the gods appeared.
Fear not. Hercules is safe.
Hylas has joined the nymphs underwater, where he is happy.
Go on your way . . . and good luck.
And so the Argonauts sailed on.
They missed their friends, but soon they would have other things to worry about . . .

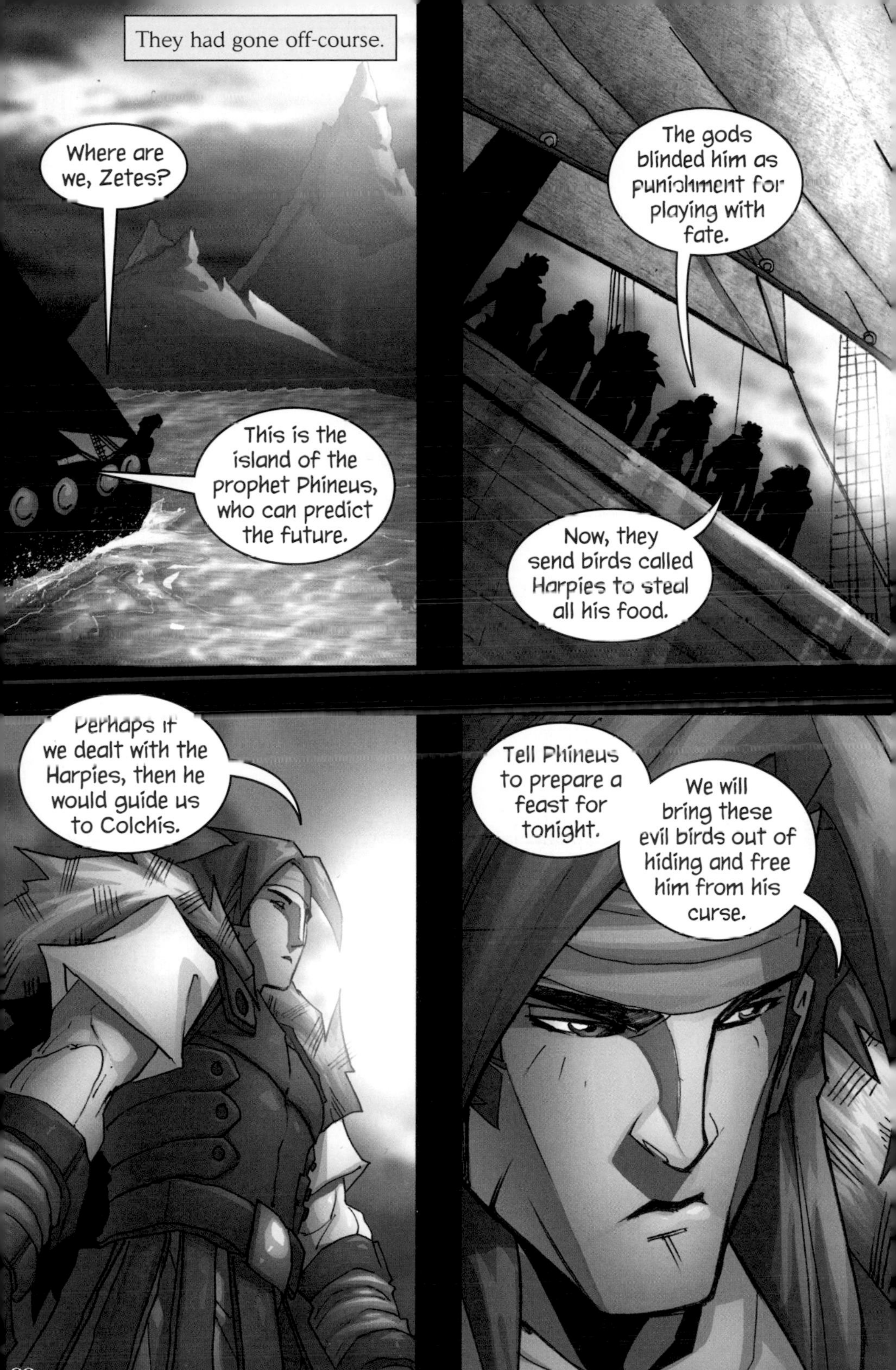
They had gone off-course.
Where are we, Zetes?
This is the island of the prophet Phineus, who can predict the future.
The gods blinded him as punishment for playing with fate.
Now, they send birds called Harpies to steal all his food.
Perhaps if we dealt with the Harpies, then he would guide us to Colchis.
Tell Phineus to prepare a feast for tonight.
We will bring these evil birds out of hiding and free him from his curse.

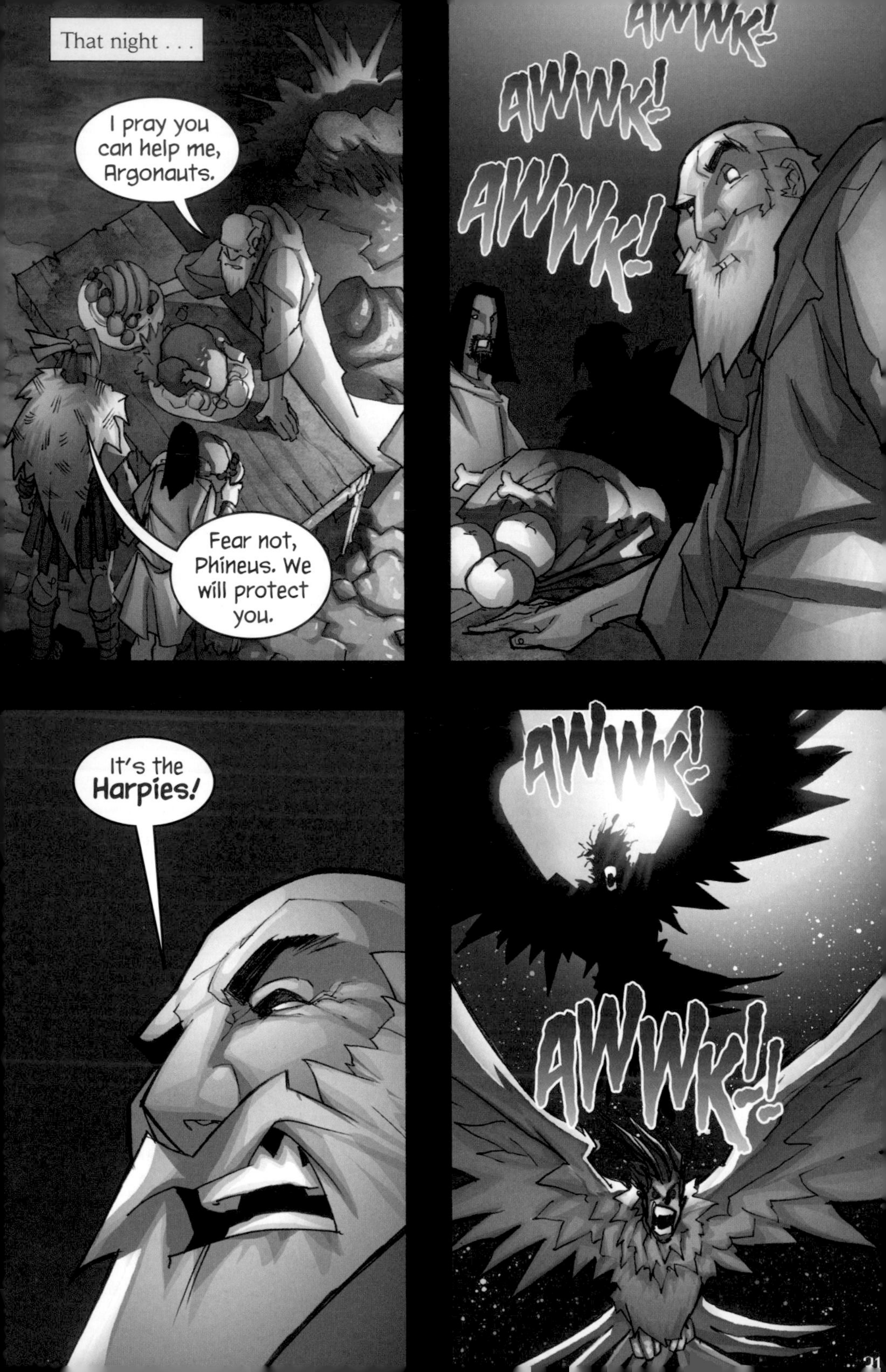
That night . . .
I pray you can help me, Argonauts.
Fear not, Phineus. We will protect you.
AWWK!
AWWK!
AWWK!
It's the Harpies!
AWWK!
AWWK!!

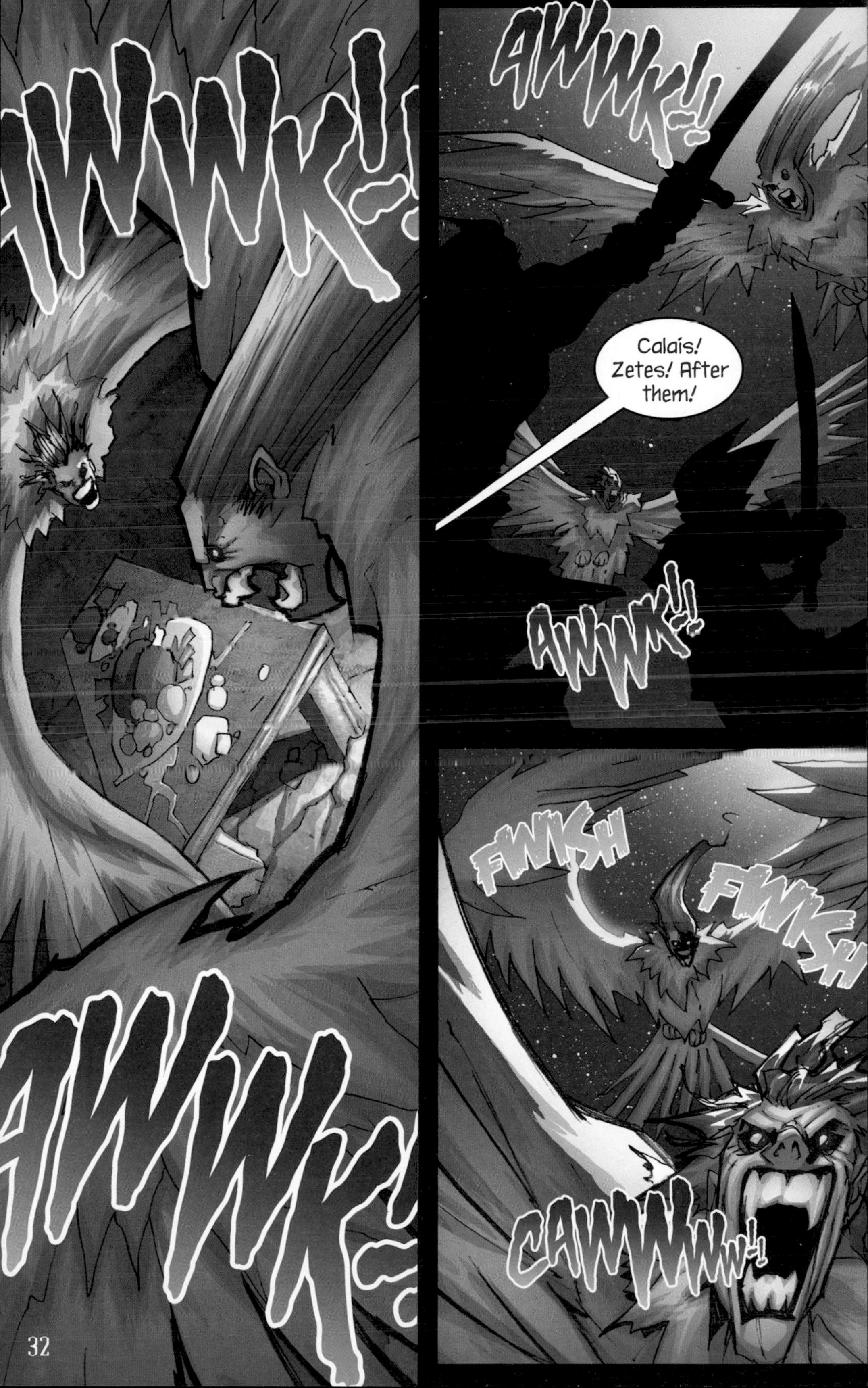
AWWK!!
AWWK!!
AWWK!!
Calais! Zetes! After them!
AWWK!!
FWISH
FWISH
CAWWWW!!

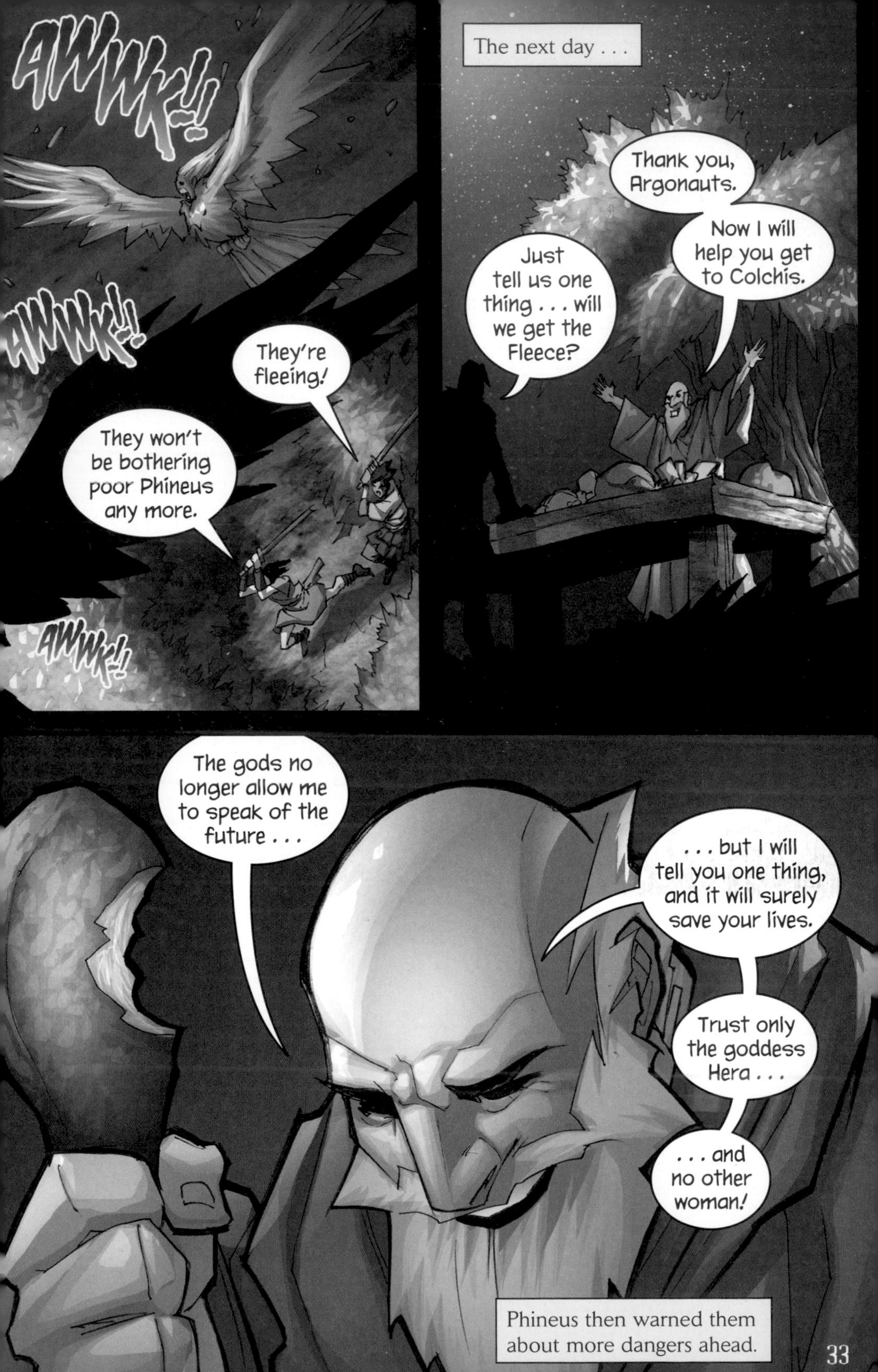
AWWK!!
AWWK!!
They're fleeing!
They won't be bothering poor Phineus any more.
AWWK!!
The next day . . .
Thank you, Argonauts.
Now I will help you get to Colchis.
Just tell us one thing . . . will we get the Fleece?
The gods no longer allow me to speak of the future . . .
. . . but I will tell you one thing, and it will surely save your lives.
Trust only the goddess Hera . . .
. . . and no other woman!
Phineus then warned them about more dangers ahead.

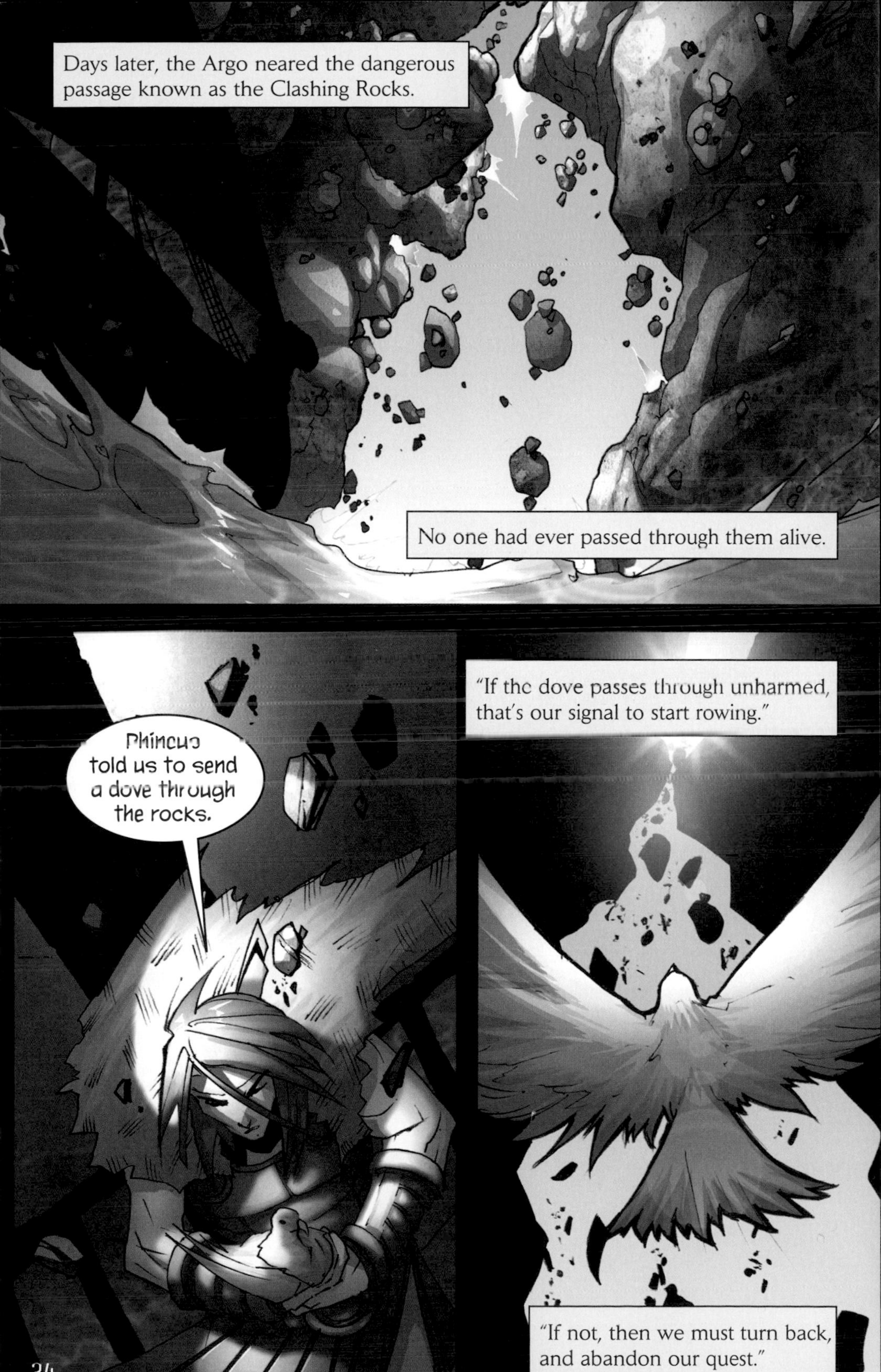
Days later, the Argo neared the dangerous passage known as the Clashing Rocks.
No one had ever passed through them alive.
Phineus told us to send a dove through the rocks.
"If the dove passes through unharmed, that's our signal to start rowing."
"If not, then we must turn back, and abandon our quest."

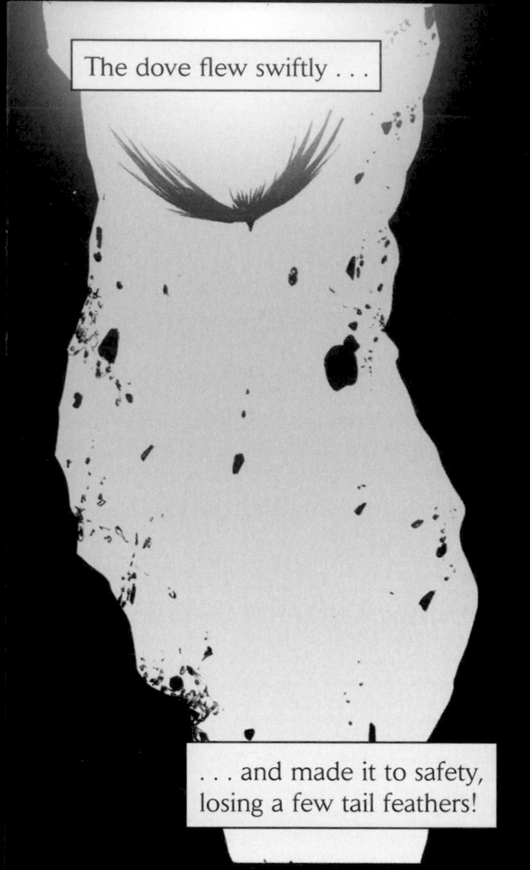
The dove flew swiftly . . .
. . . and made it to safety, losing a few tail feathers!

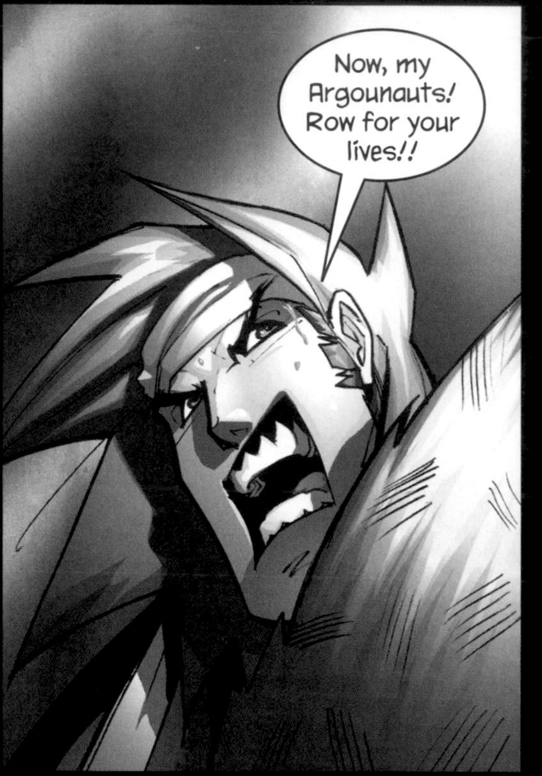
Now, my Argounauts! Row for your lives!!

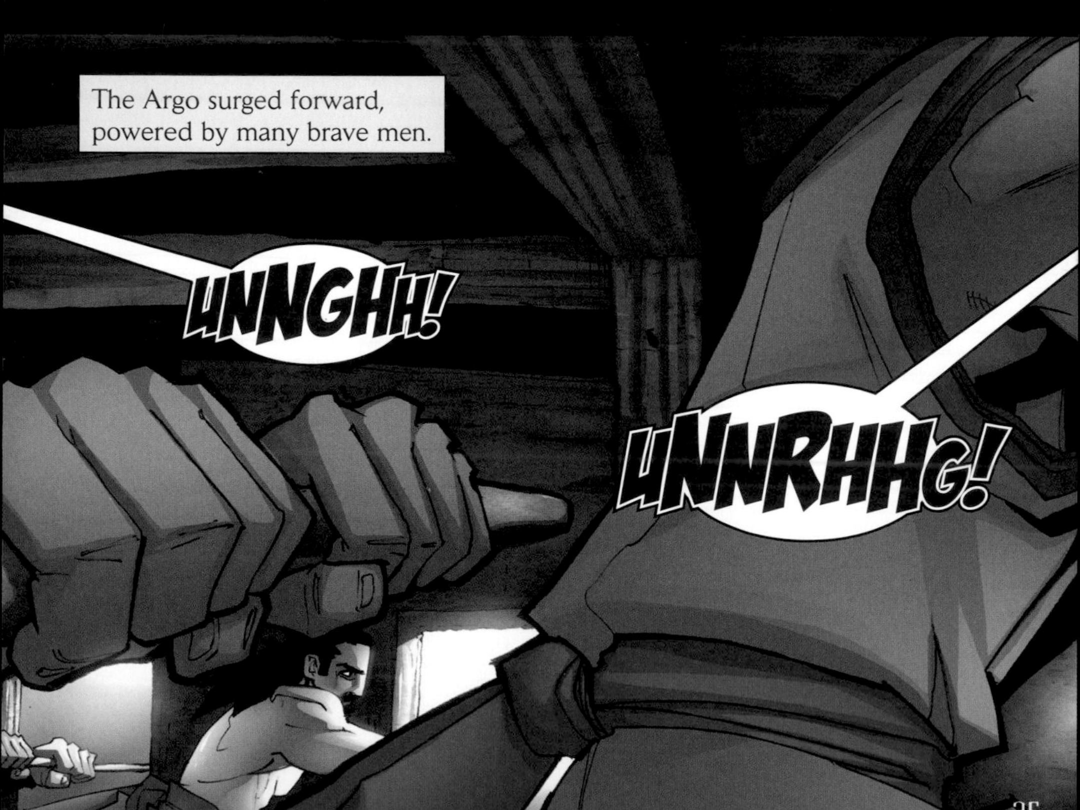
The Argo surged forward, powered by many brave men.
UNNGHH!
UNNRHHG!

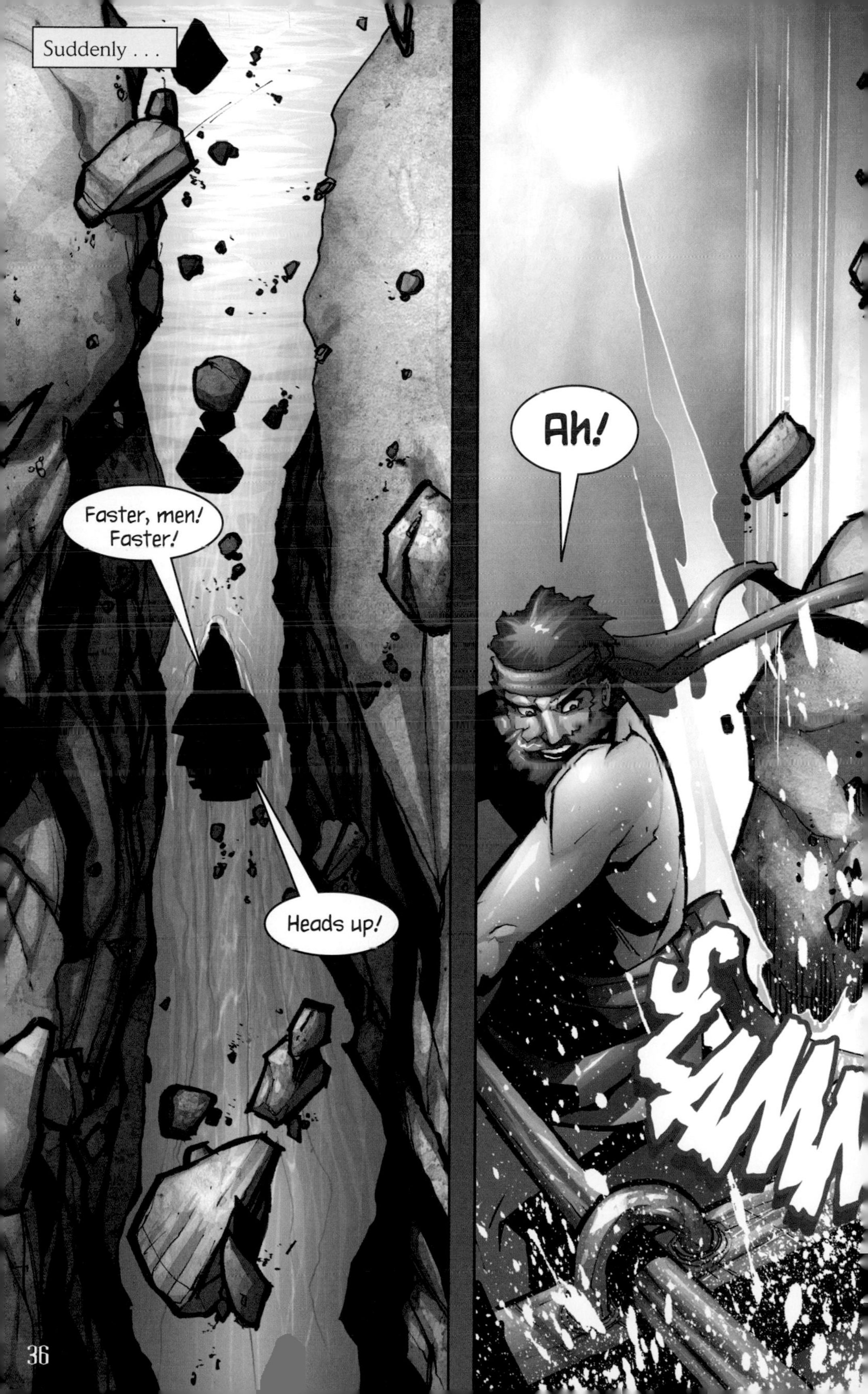
Suddenly . . .
Faster, men! Faster!
Heads up!
Ah!

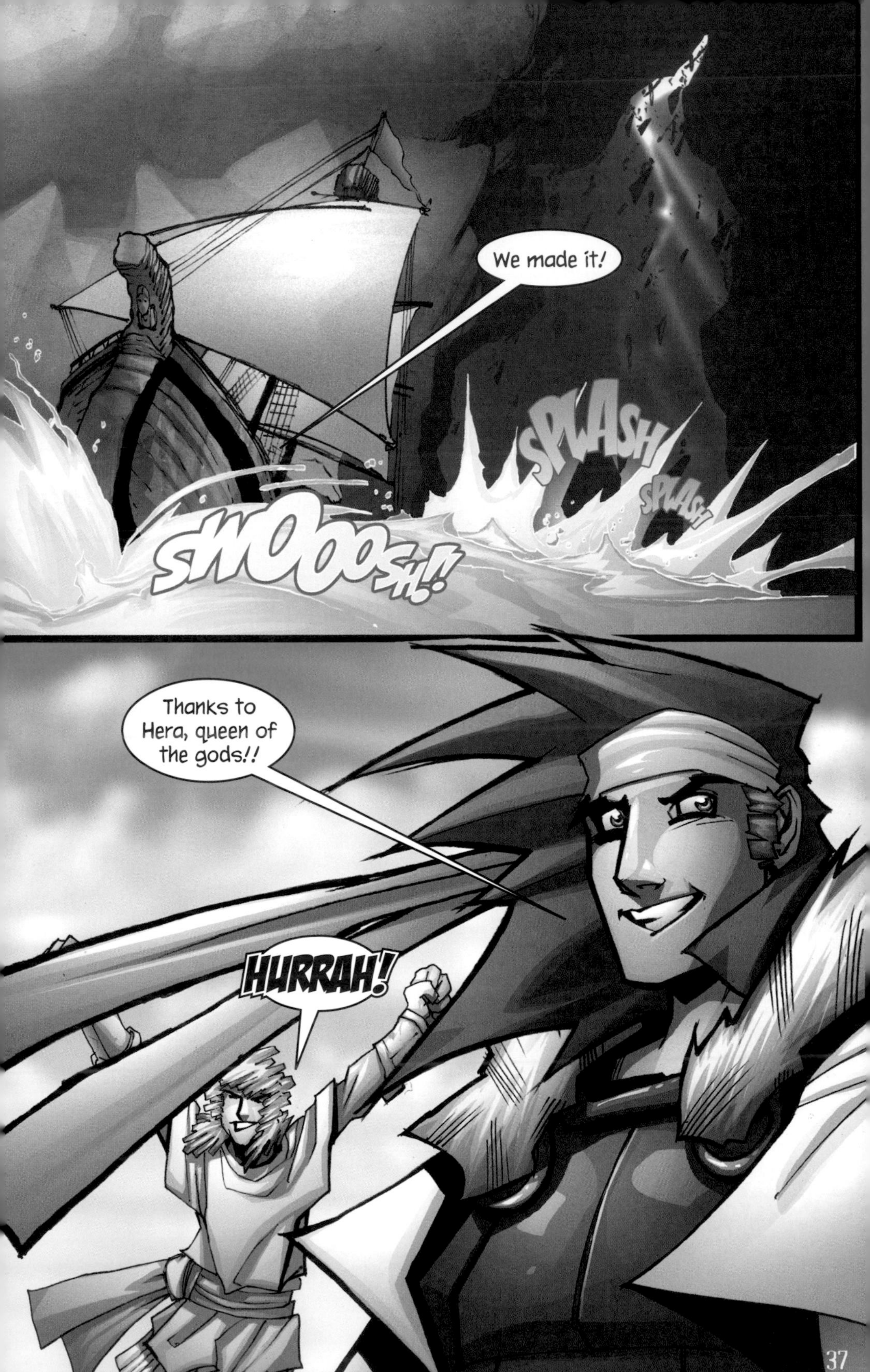

We made it!
SPLASH
SPLASH
SWOOOSH!!
Thanks to Hera, queen of the gods!!
HURRAH!

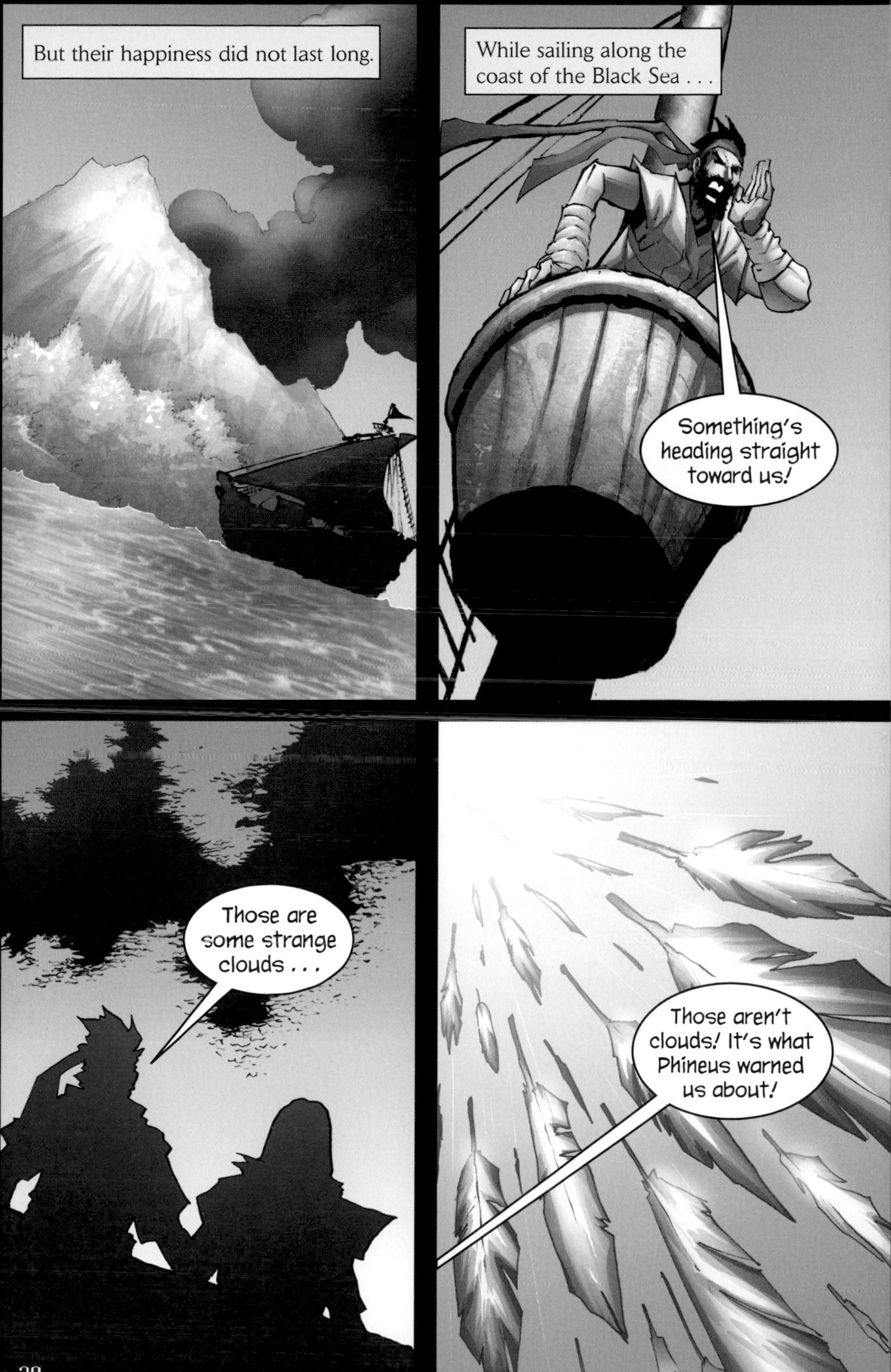
But their happiness did not last long.
While sailing along the coast of the Black Sea . . .
Something's heading straight toward us!
Those are some strange clouds . . .
Those aren't clouds! It's what Phineus warned us about!

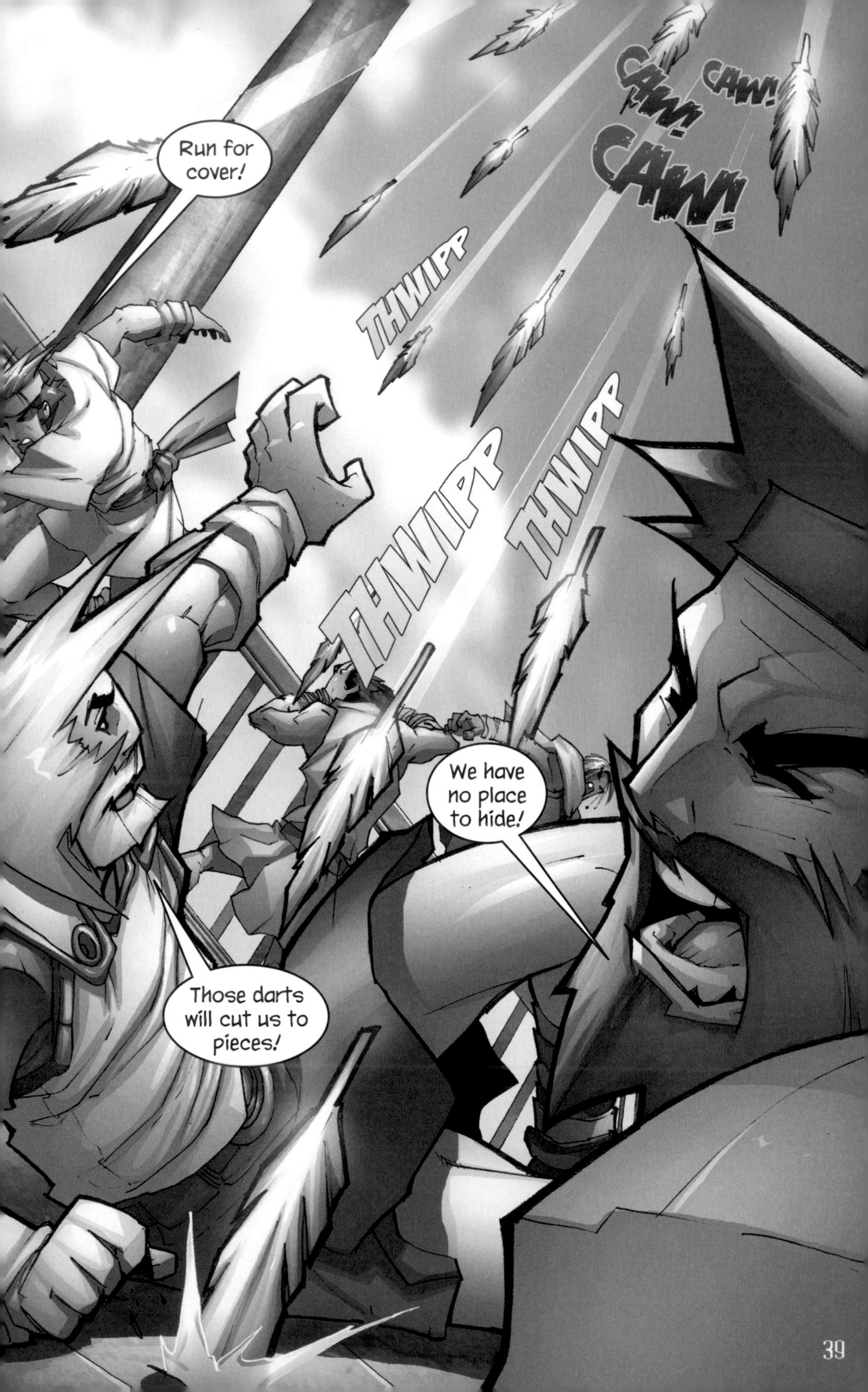
Run for cover!
CAW!
CAW!
CAW!
THWIPP
THWIPP
THWIPP
We have no place to hide!
Those darts will cut us to pieces!

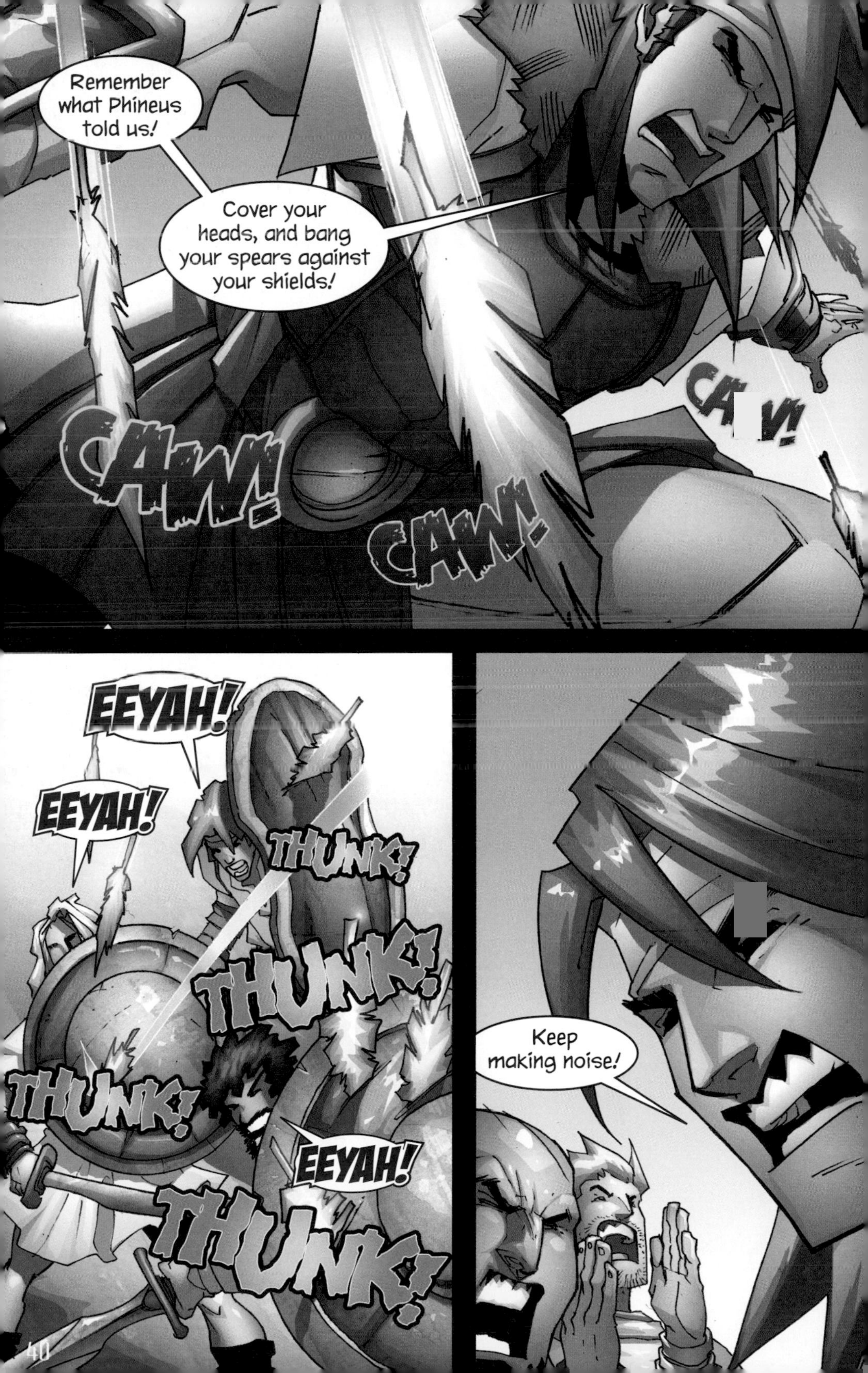
Remember what Phineus told us!
Cover your heads, and bang your spears against your shields!
CAW!
CAW!
EEYAH!
EEYAH!
THUNK!
THUNK!
THUNK!
EEYAH!
THUNK!
Keep making noise!

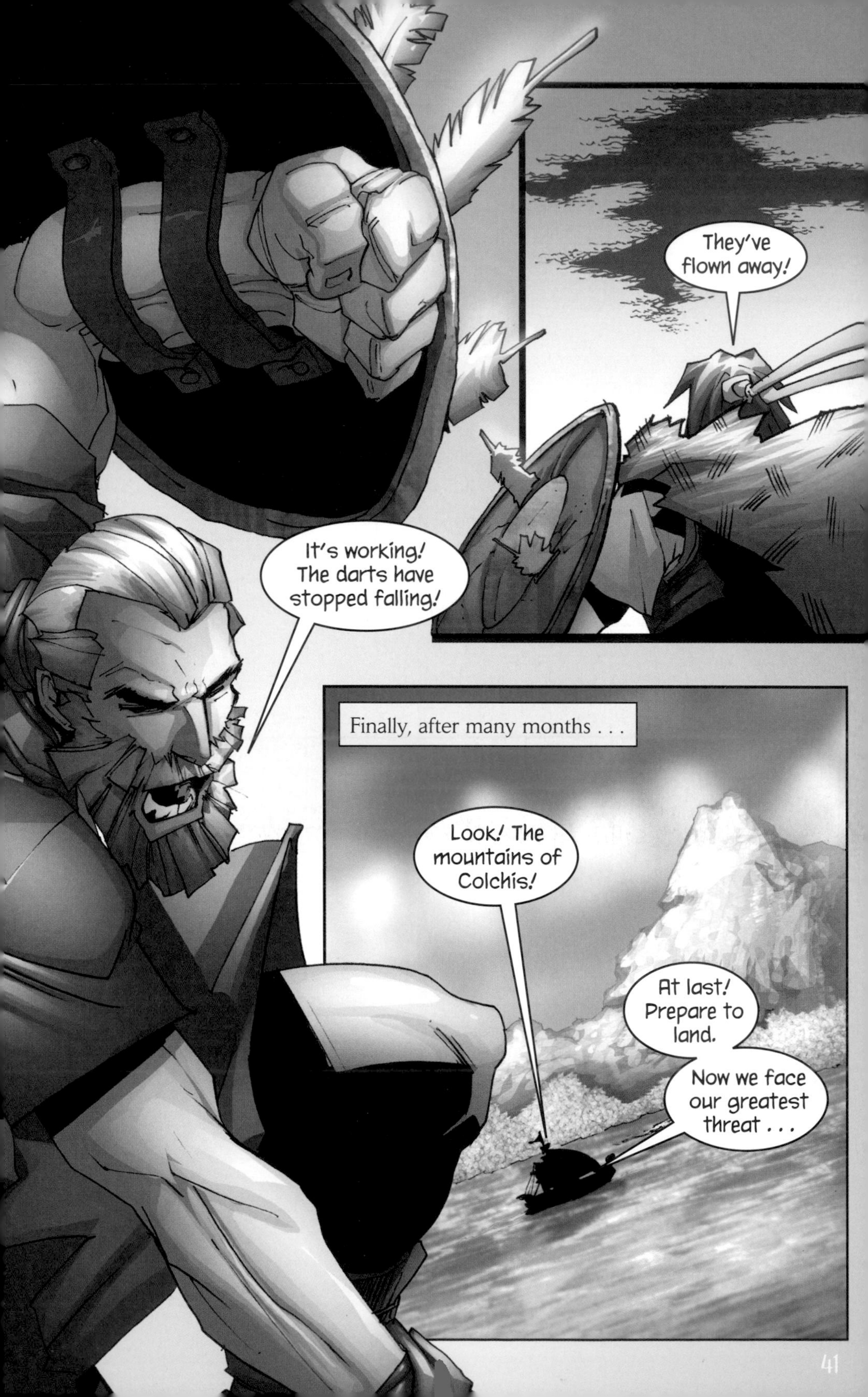
It's working! The darts have stopped falling!
They've flown away!
Finally, after many months . . .
Look! The mountains of Colchis!
At last! Prepare to land.
Now we face our greatest threat . . .

CHAPTER 4: MEDEA'S MAGIC

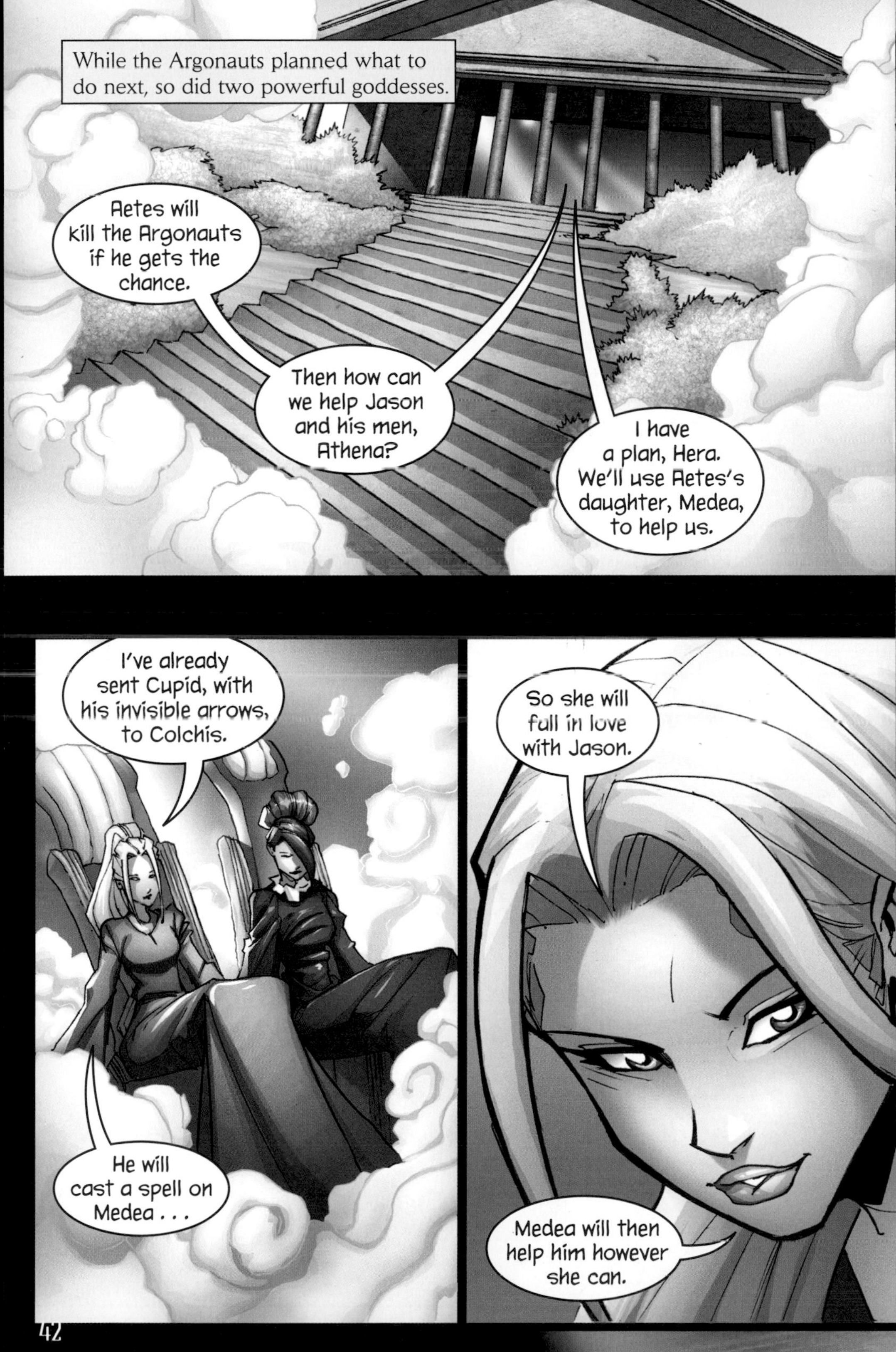
While the Argonauts planned what to do next, so did two powerful goddesses.
Aetes will kill the Argonauts if he gets the chance.
Then how can we help Jason and his men, Athena?
I have a plan, Hera. We'll use Aetes's daughter, Medea, to help us.
I've already sent Cupid, with his invisible arrows, to Colchis.
He will cast a spell on Medea . . .
So she will fall in love with Jason.
Medea will then help him however she can.

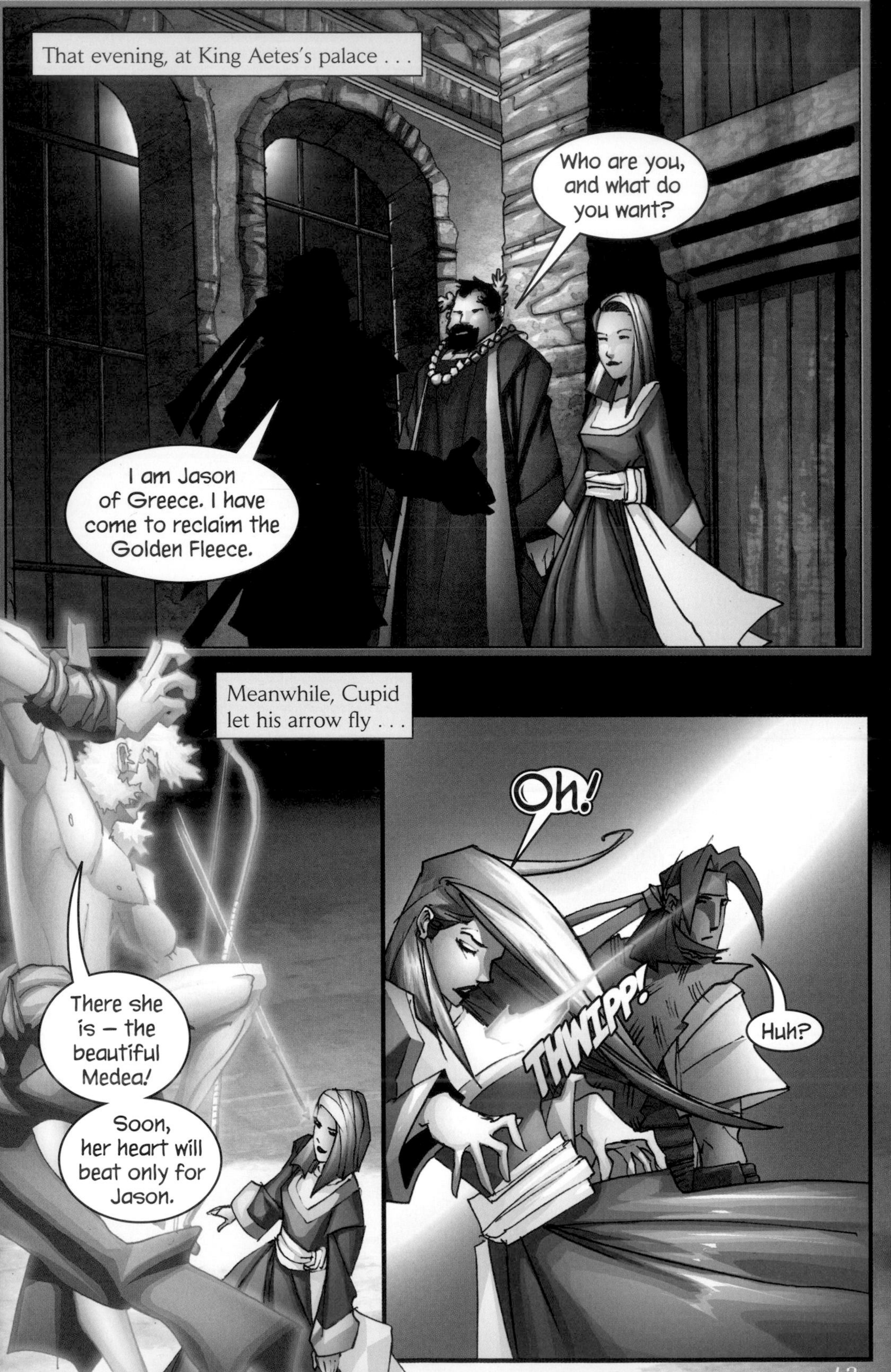
That evening, at King Aetes's palace . . .
Who are you, and what do you want?
I am Jason of Greece. I have come to reclaim the Golden Fleece.
Meanwhile, Cupid let his arrow fly . . .
There she is — the beautiful Medea!
Soon, her heart will beat only for Jason.
Oh!
THWIPP!
Huh?

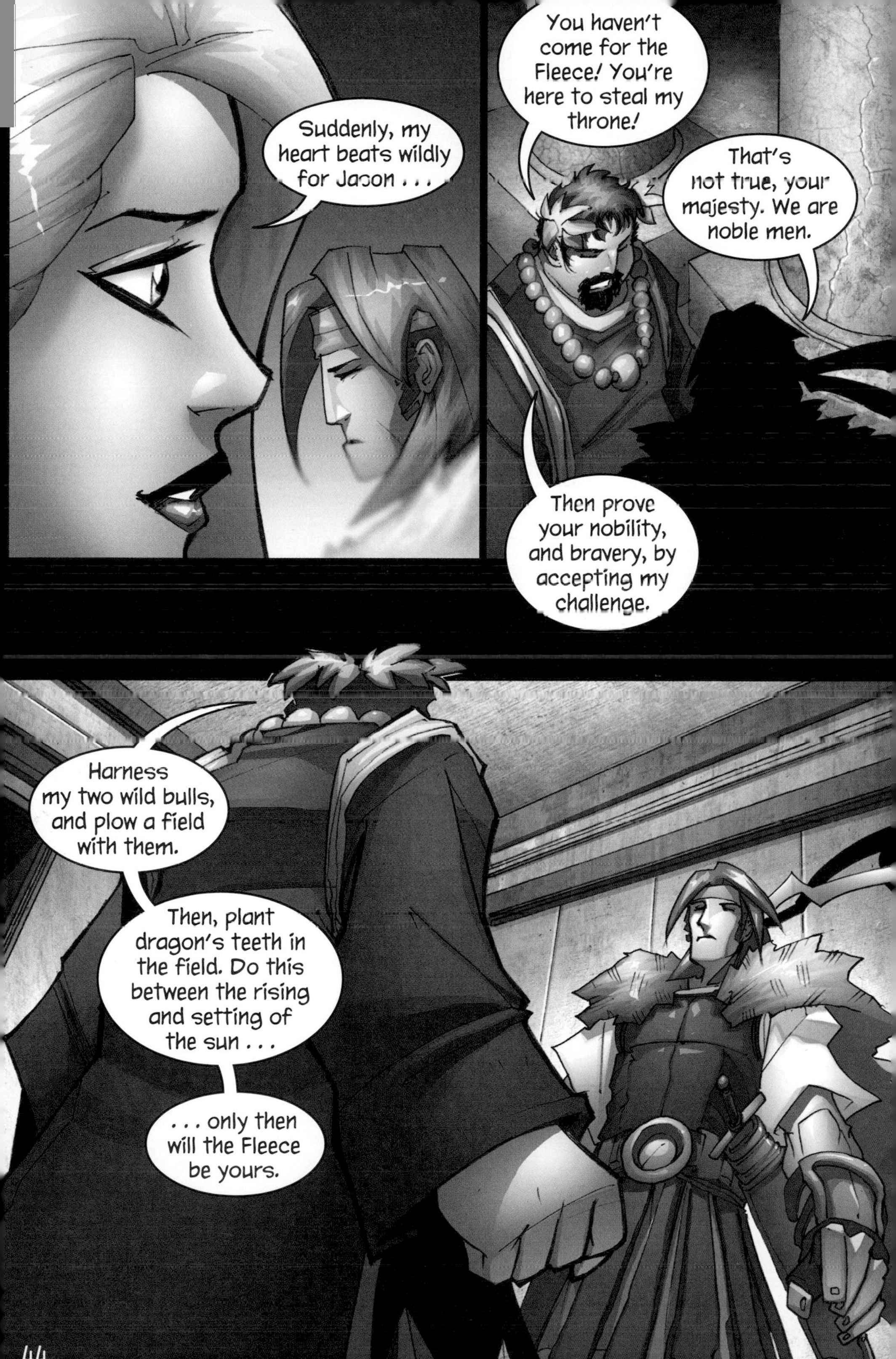
Suddenly, my heart beats wildly for Jason . . .
You haven't come for the Fleece! You're here to steal my throne!
That's not true, your majesty. We are noble men.
Then prove your nobility, and bravery, by accepting my challenge.
Harness my two wild bulls, and plow a field with them.
Then, plant dragon's teeth in the field. Do this between the rising and setting of the sun . . .
. . . only then will the Fleece be yours.

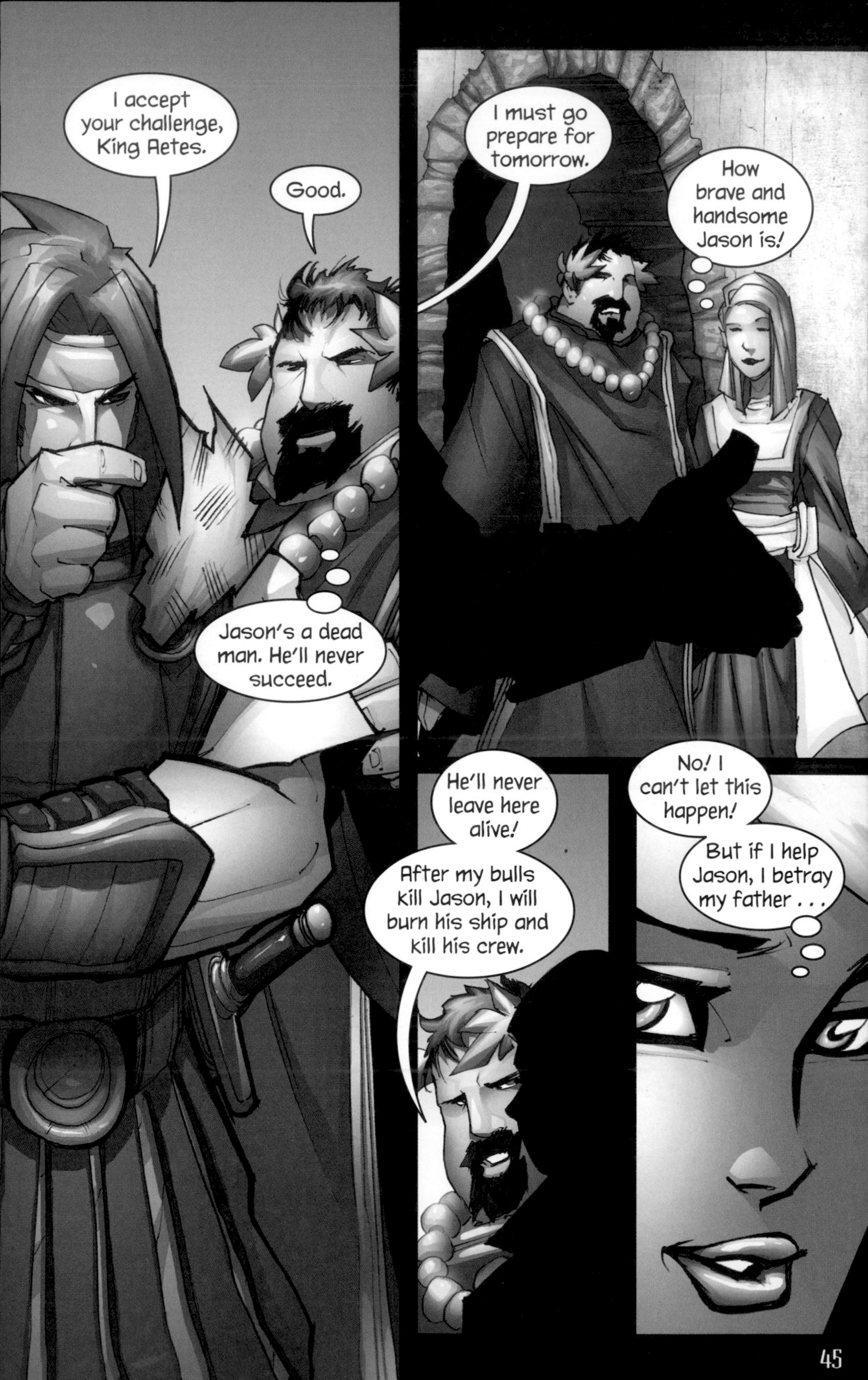
I accept your challenge, King Aetes.
Good.
Jason's a dead man. He'll never succeed.
I must go prepare for tomorrow.
How brave and handsome Jason is!
He'll never leave here alive!
After my bulls kill Jason, I will burn his ship and kill his crew.
No! I can't let this happen!
But if I help Jason, I betray my father . . .

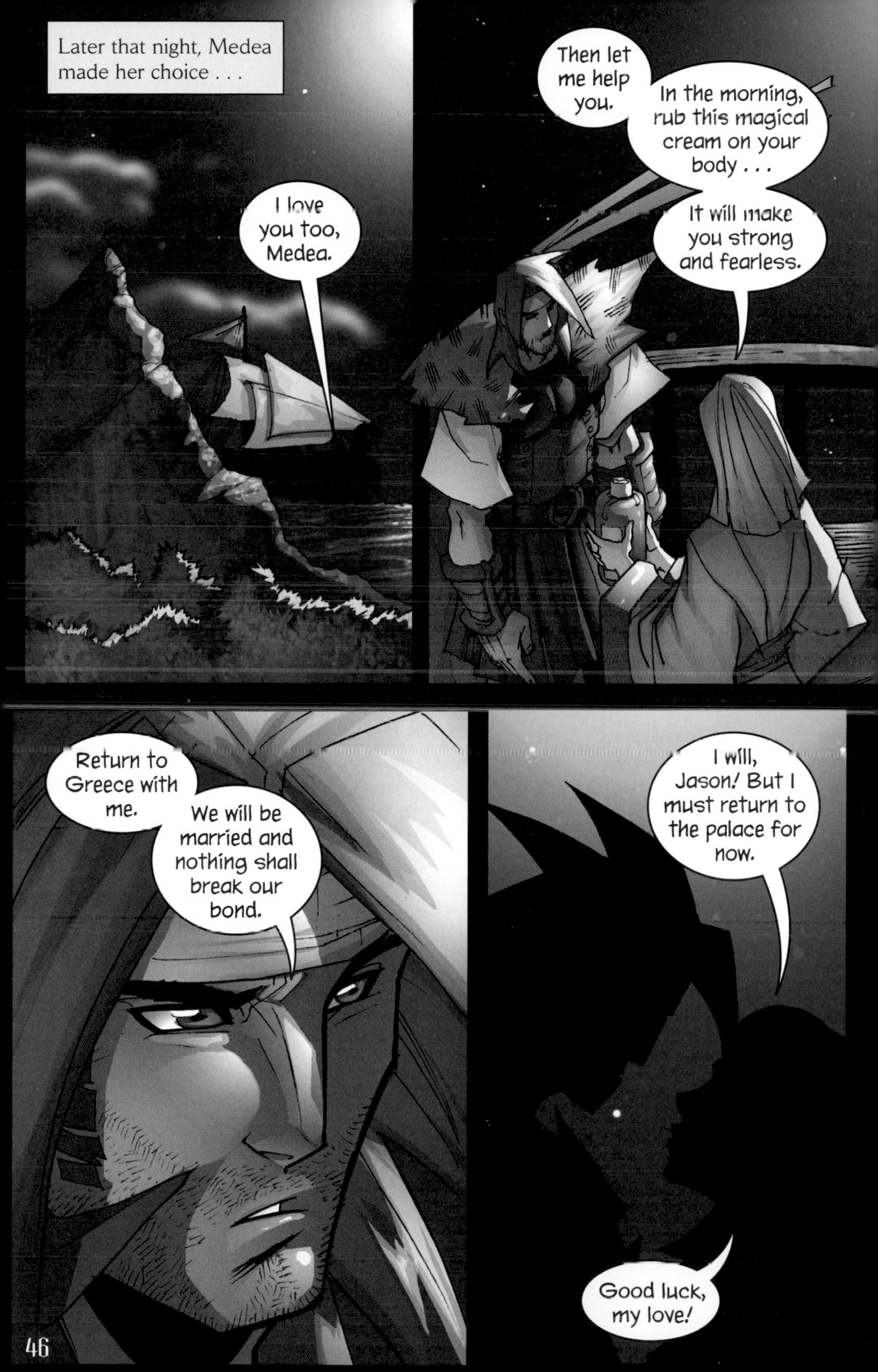

Later that night, Medea made her choice . . .
I love you too, Medea.
Then let me help you.
In the morning, rub this magical cream on your body . . .
It will make you strong and fearless.
Return to Greece with me.
We will be married and nothing shall break our bond.
I will, Jason! But I must return to the palace for now.
Good luck, my love!

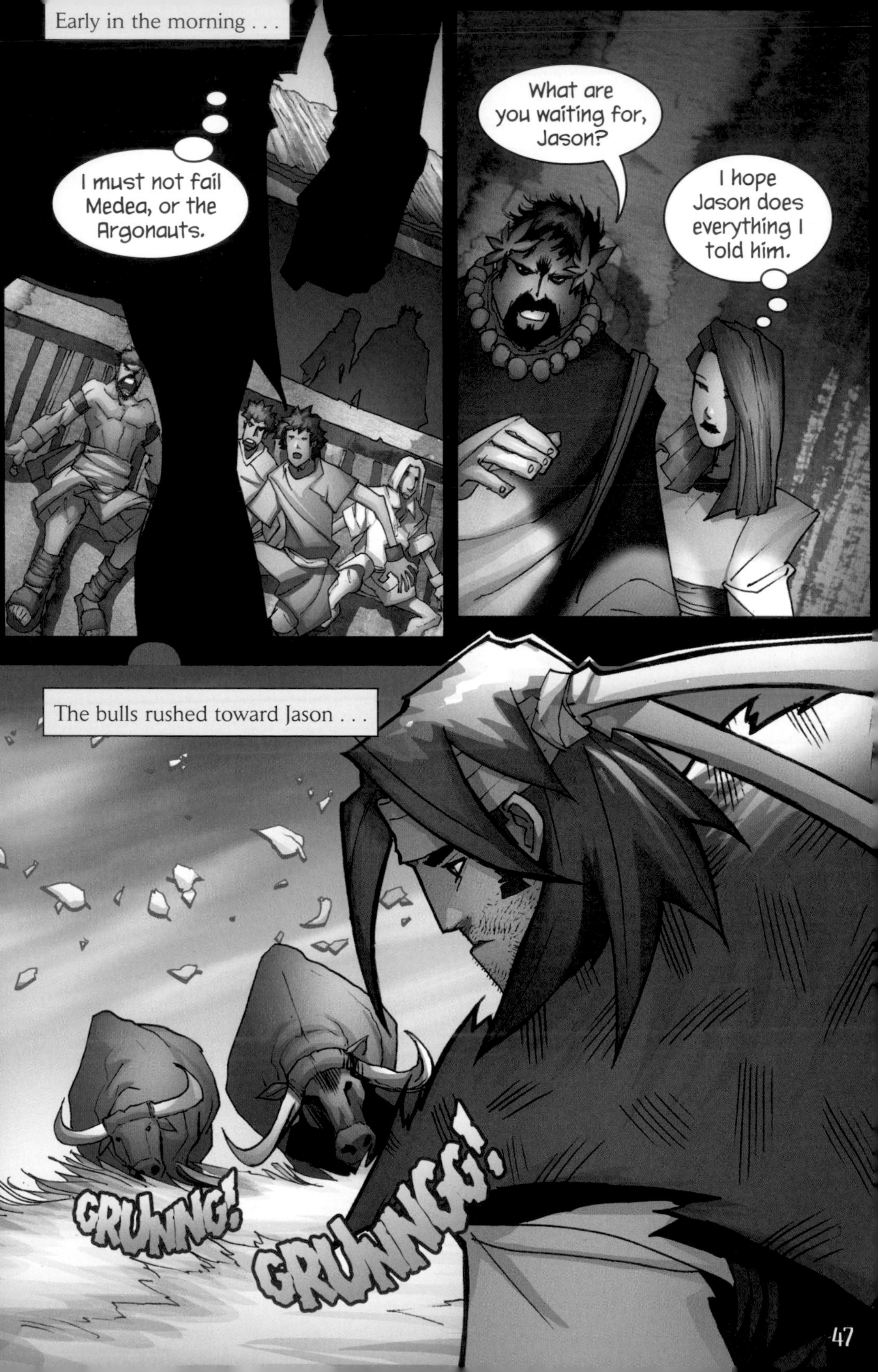
Early in the morning . . .
I must not fail Medea, or the Argonauts.
What are you waiting for, Jason?
I hope Jason does everything I told him.
The bulls rushed toward Jason . . .
GRUNNG!
GRUNNGG!

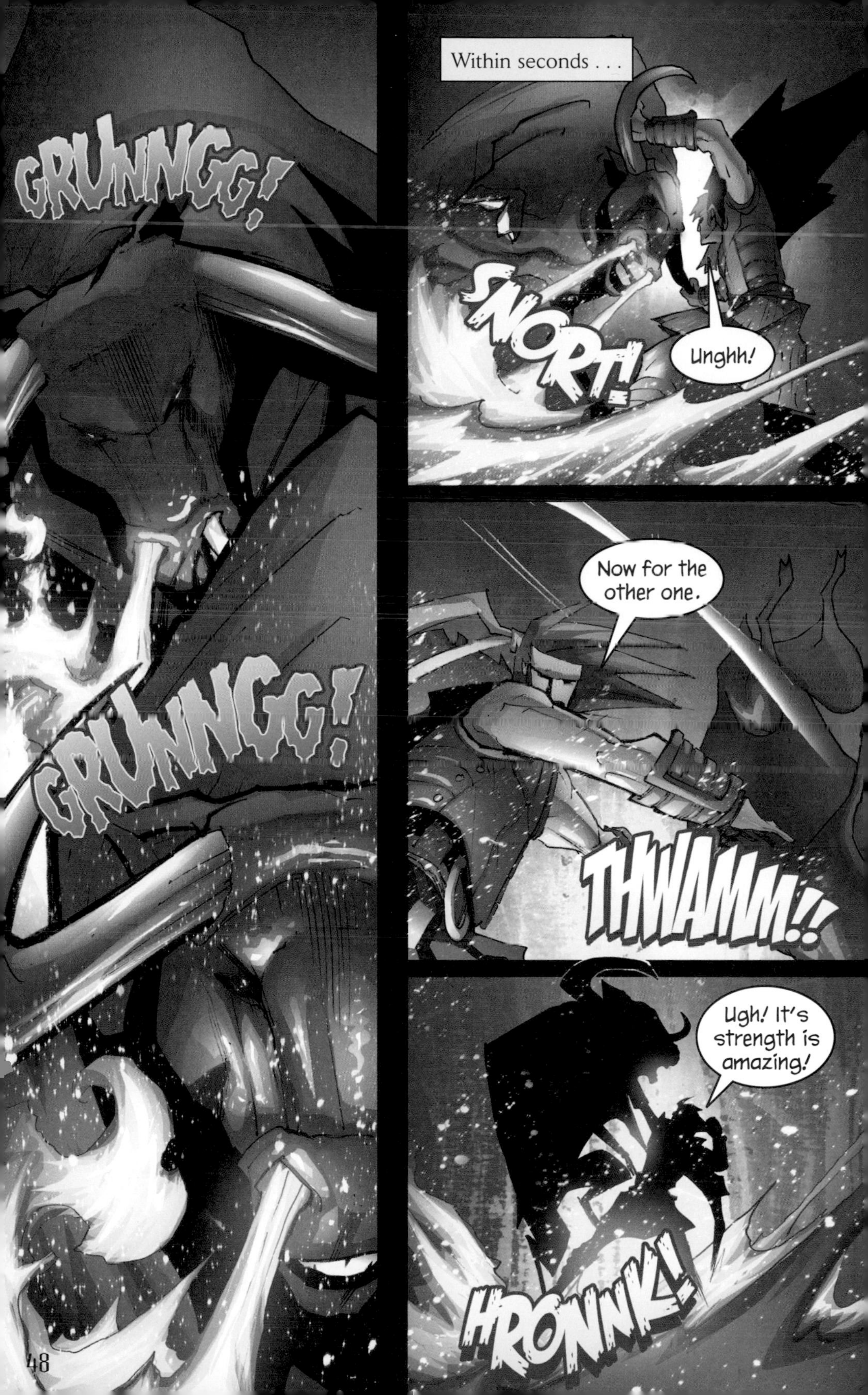

GRUNNGG!
GRUNNGG!
Within seconds . . .
SNORT!
Unghh!
Now for the other one.
THWAMM!!
Ugh! It's strength is amazing!
HRONNK!

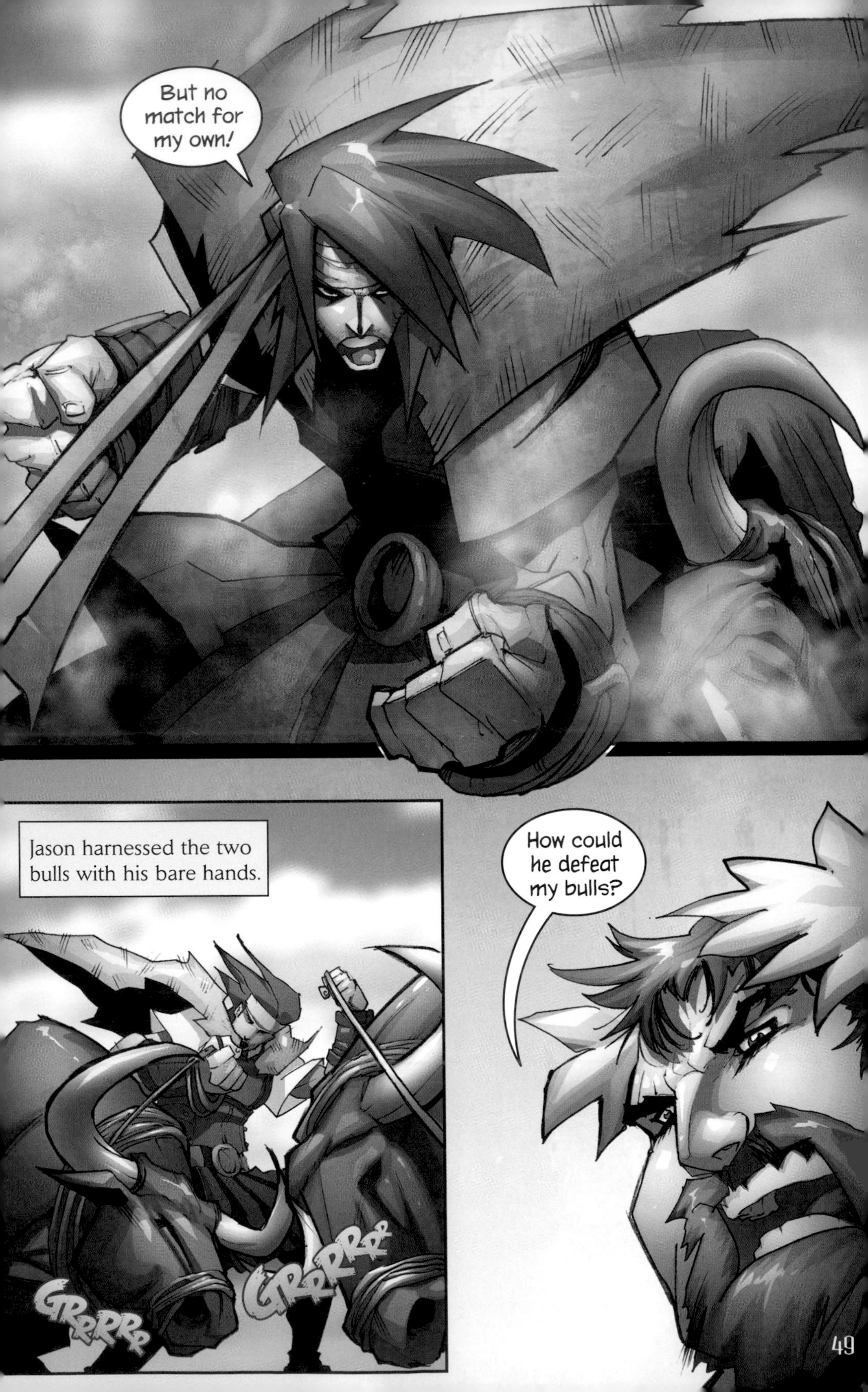
But no match for my own!
Jason harnessed the two bulls with his bare hands.
GRRRRR
GRRRRR
How could he defeat my bulls?

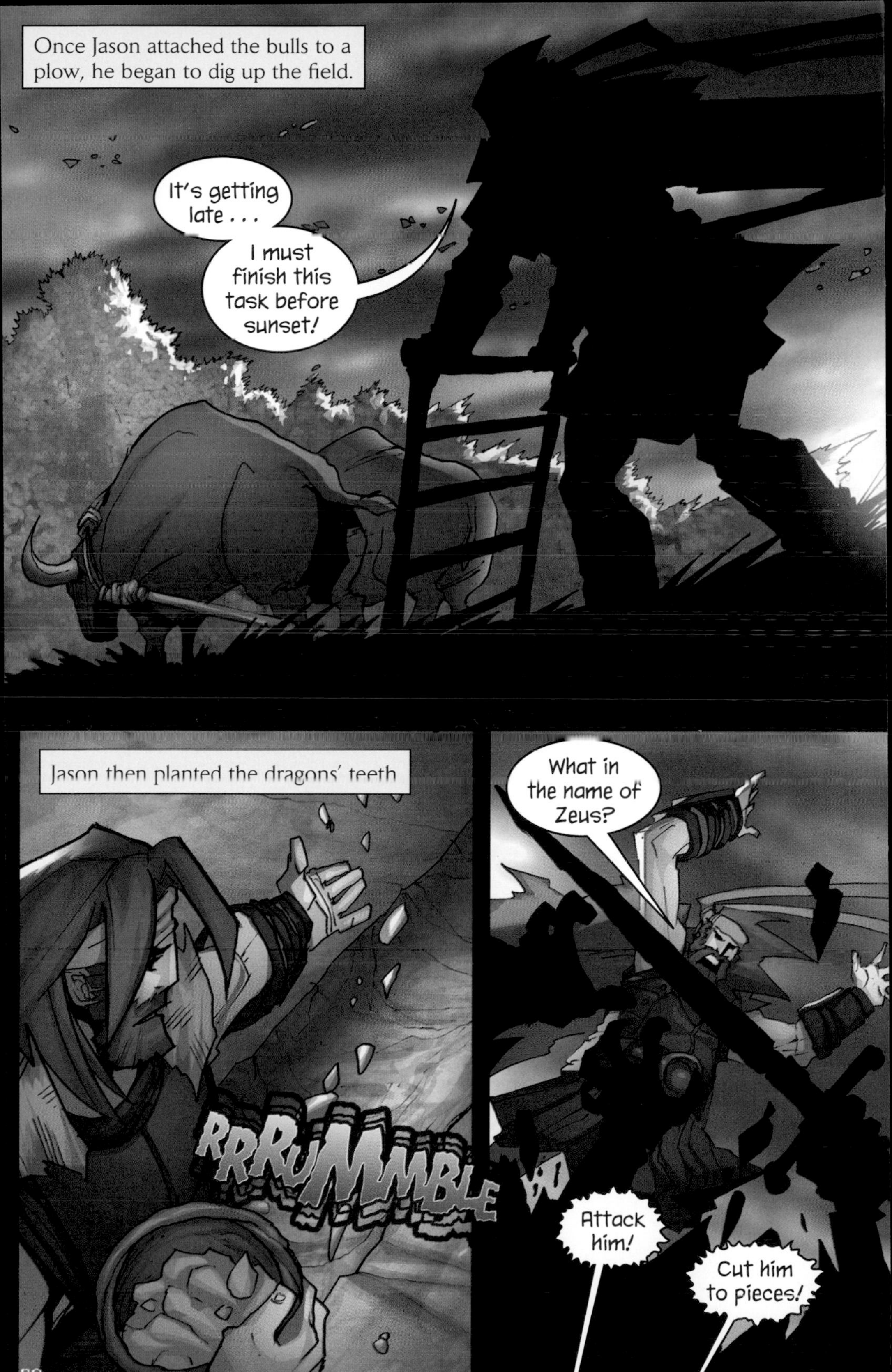

Once Jason attached the bulls to a plow, he began to dig up the field.
It's getting late . . .
I must finish this task before sunset!
Jason then planted the dragons' teeth
RRRUMMMBLE
What in the name of Zeus?
Attack him!
Cut him to pieces!

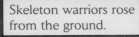

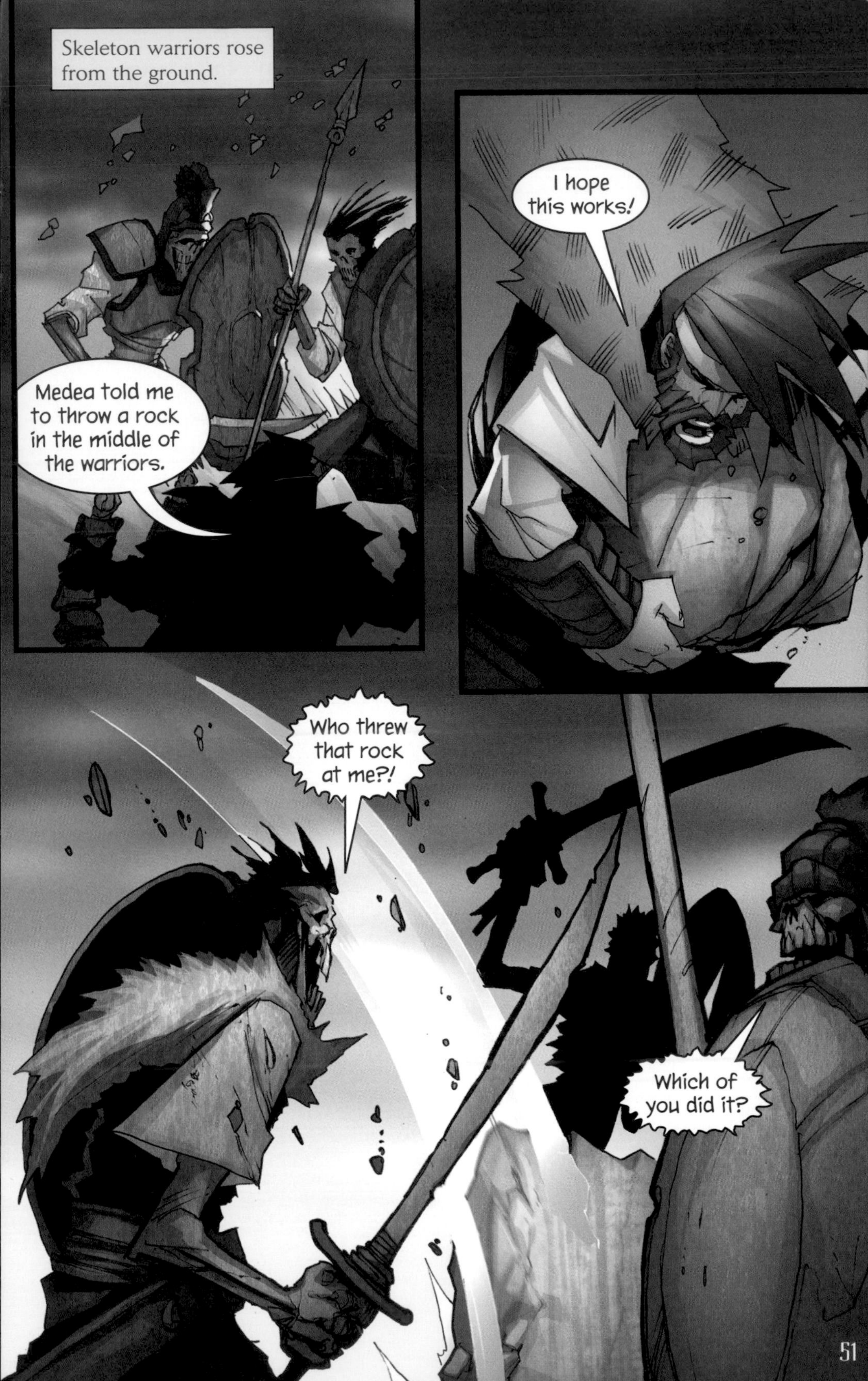

Skeleton warriors rose from the ground.

Medea told me to throw a rock in the middle of the warriors.

I hope this works!

Who threw that rock at me?!

Which of you did it?

51

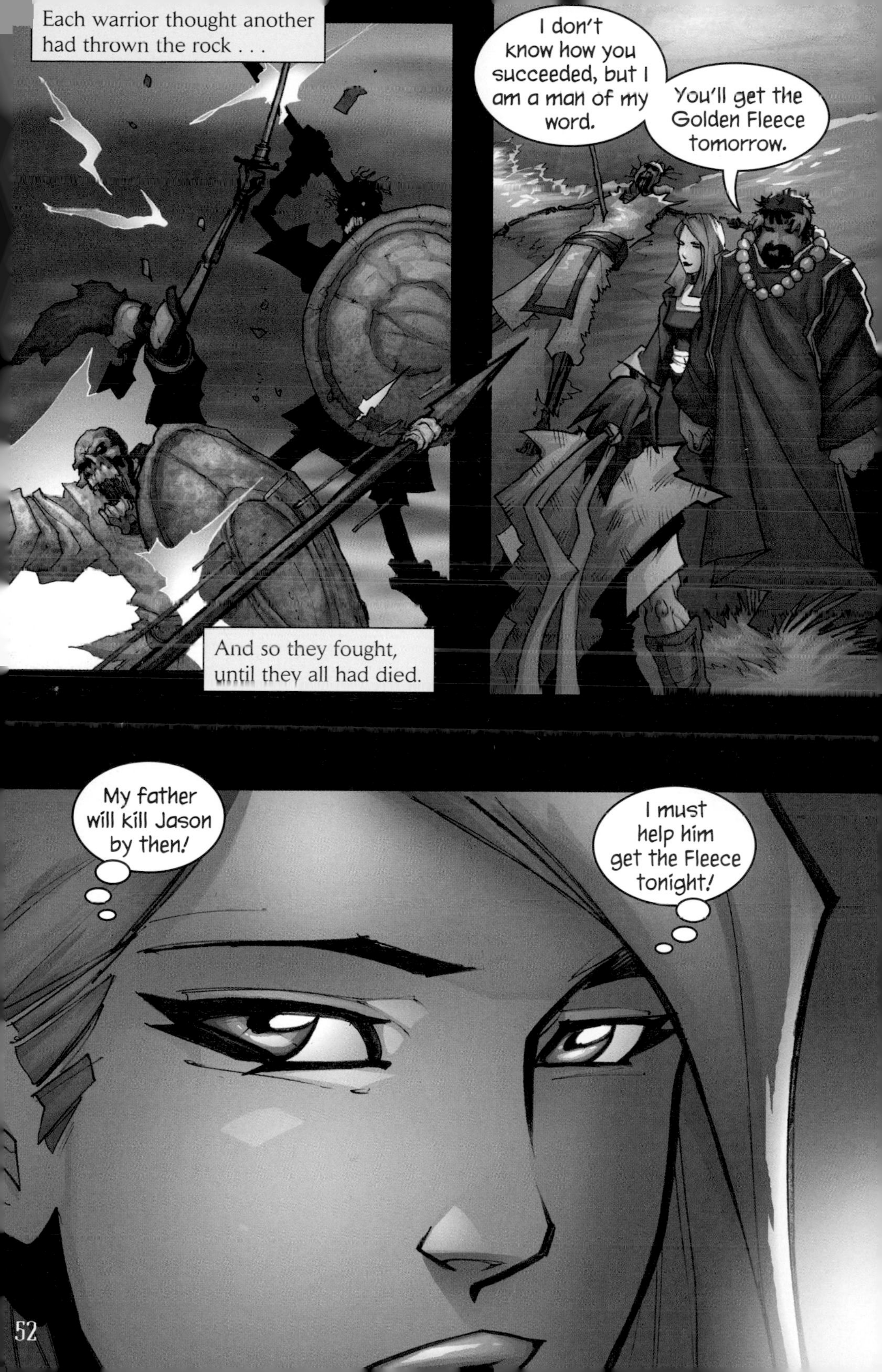

Each warrior thought another had thrown the rock . . .
And so they fought, until they all had died.
I don't know how you succeeded, but I am a man of my word.
You'll get the Golden Fleece tomorrow.
My father will kill Jason by then!
I must help him get the Fleece tonight!

Later that night, Medea told Jason about her father's plan to kill him.

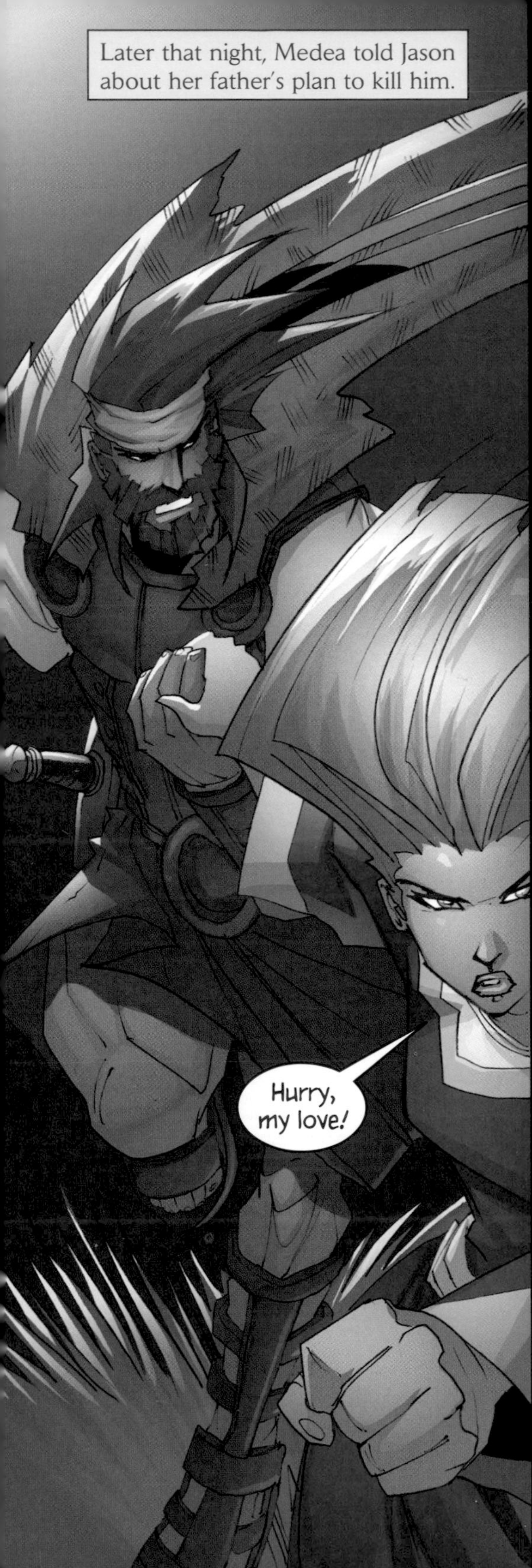
Hurry, my love!

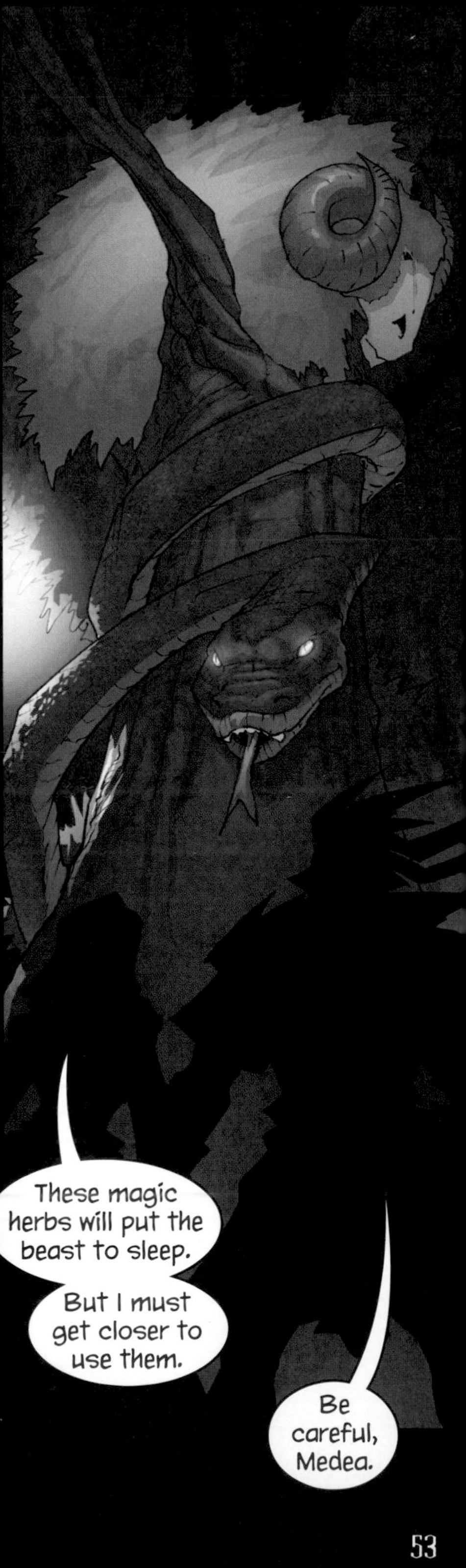
These magic herbs will put the beast to sleep.
But I must get closer to use them.
Be careful, Medea.

CHAPTER 5: CAPTURING THE FLEECE

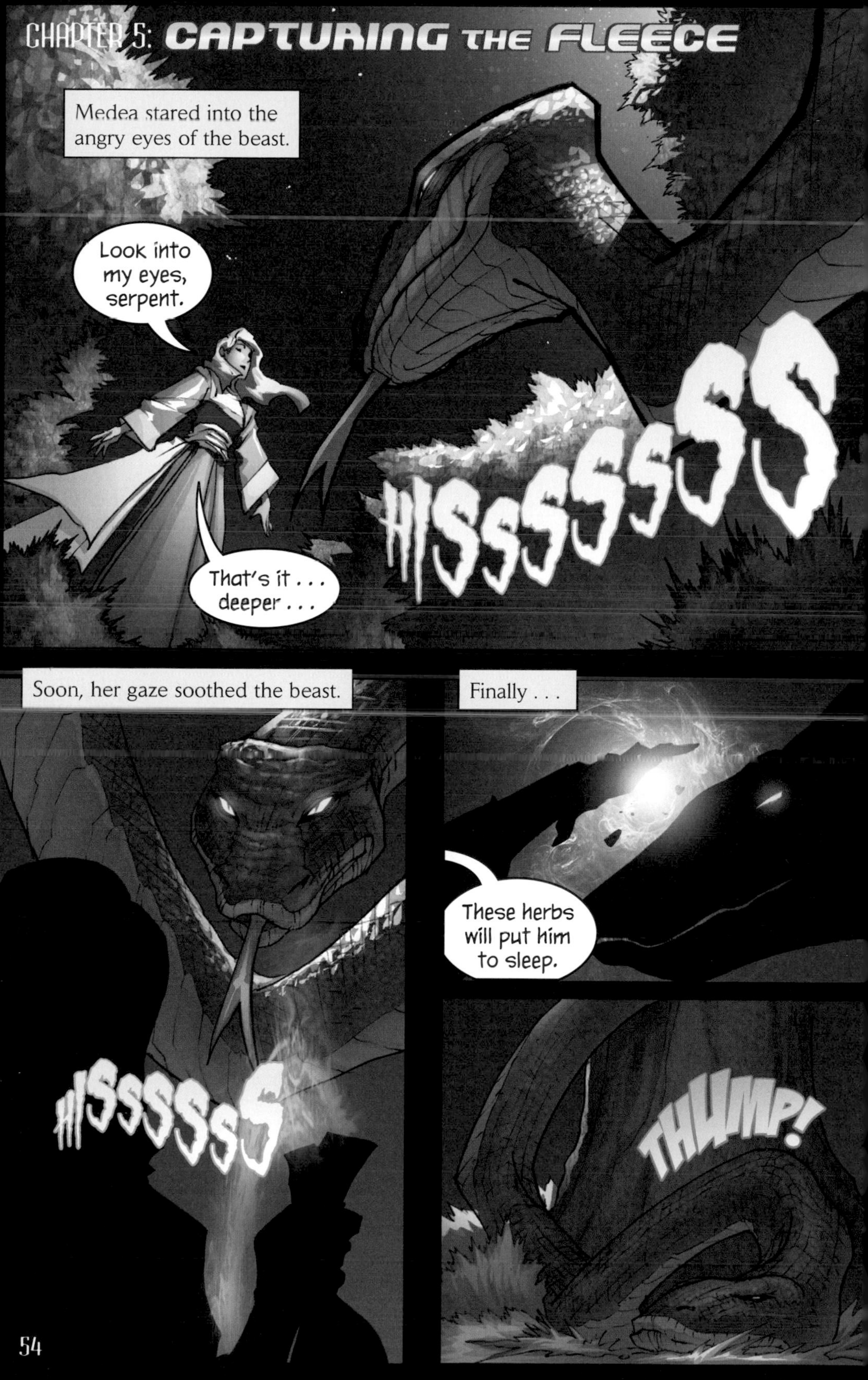

Medea stared into the angry eyes of the beast.
Look into my eyes, serpent.
HISSSSSSS
That's it . . . deeper . . .
Soon, her gaze soothed the beast.
HISSSSSS
Finally . . .
These herbs will put him to sleep.
THUMP!

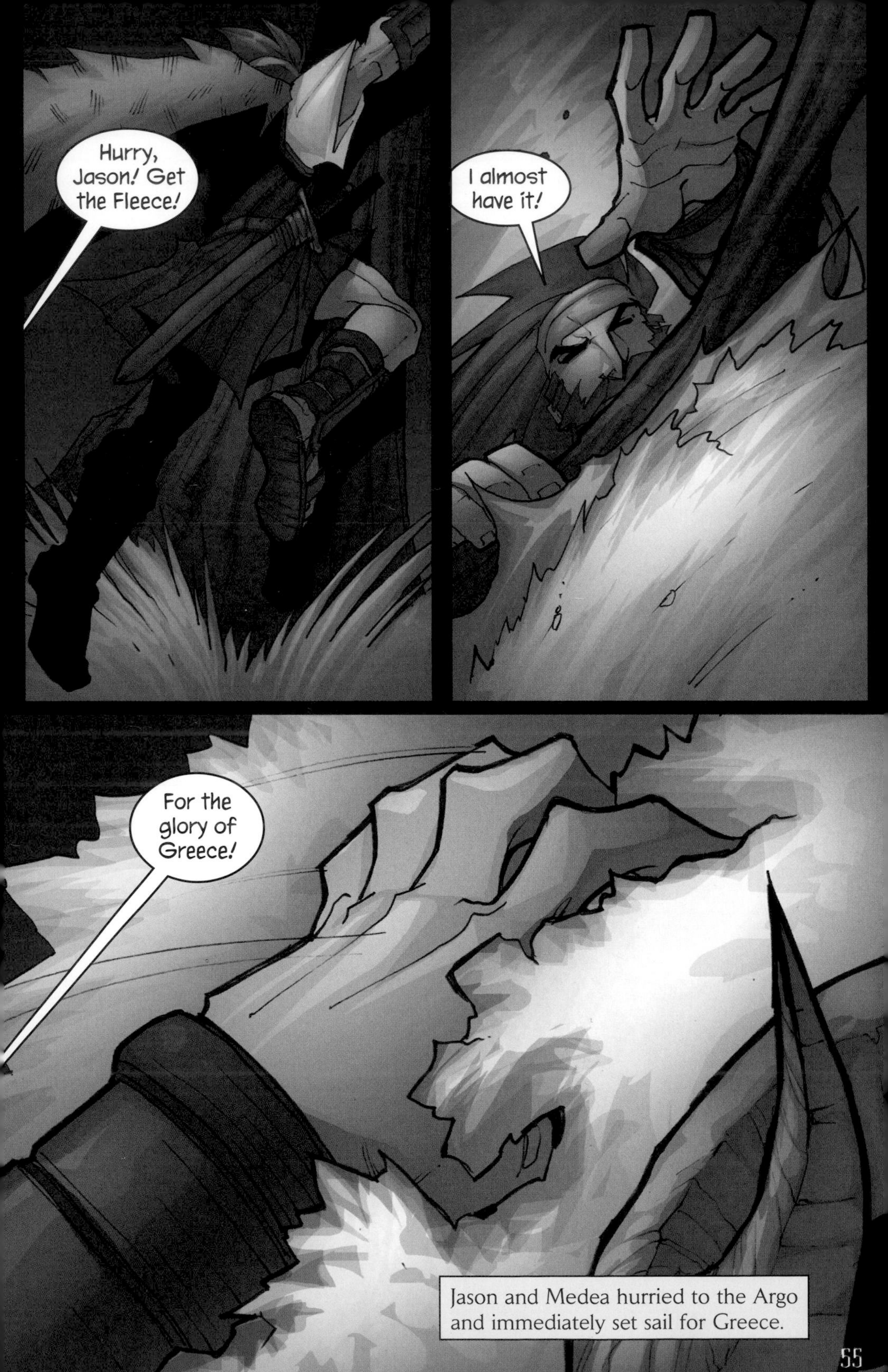
Hurry, Jason! Get the Fleece!
I almost have it!
For the glory of Greece!
Jason and Medea hurried to the Argo and immediately set sail for Greece.

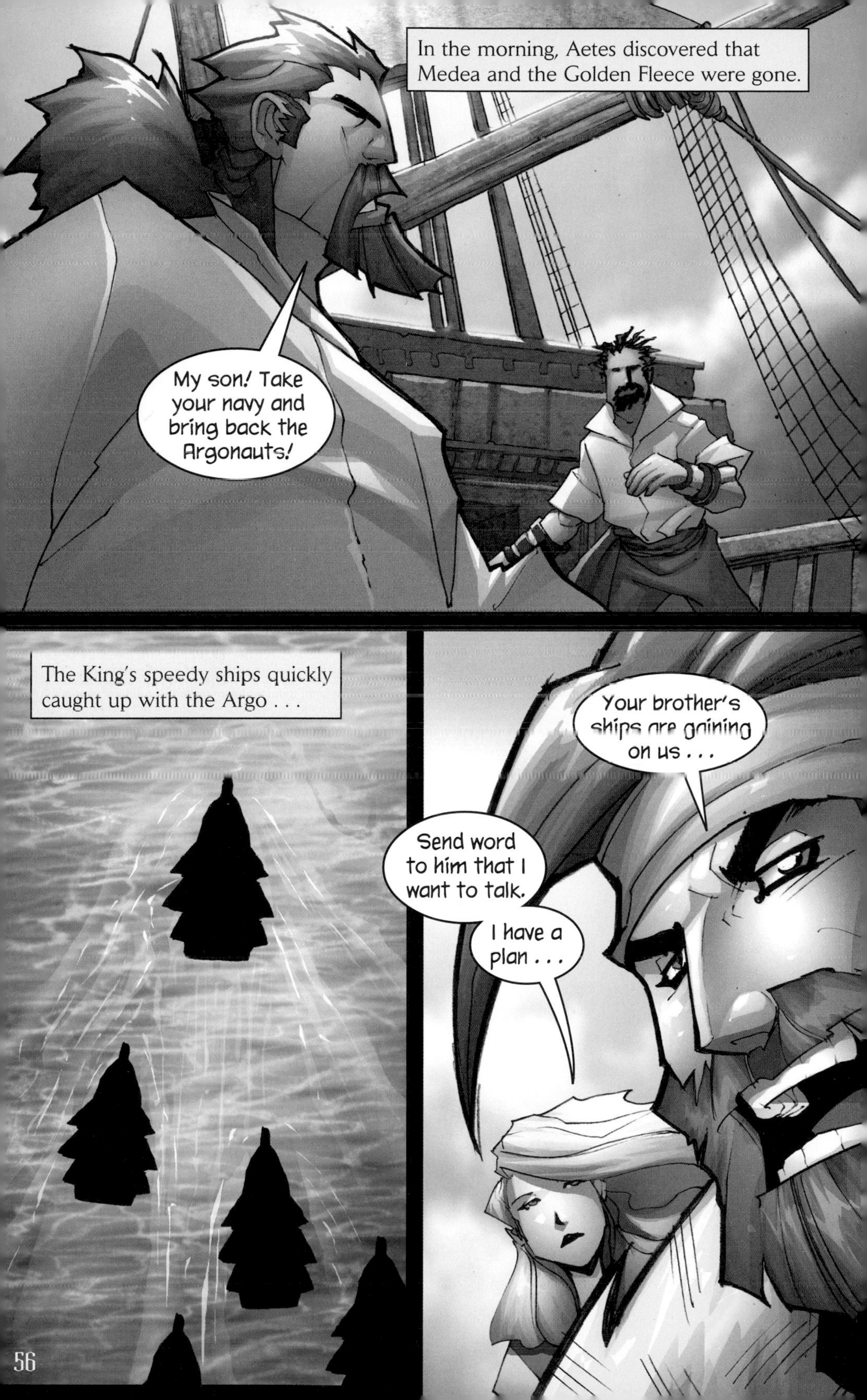
In the morning, Aetes discovered that Medea and the Golden Fleece were gone.
My son! Take your navy and bring back the Argonauts!
The King's speedy ships quickly caught up with the Argo . . .
Your brother's ships are gaining on us . . .
Send word to him that I want to talk.
I have a plan . . .

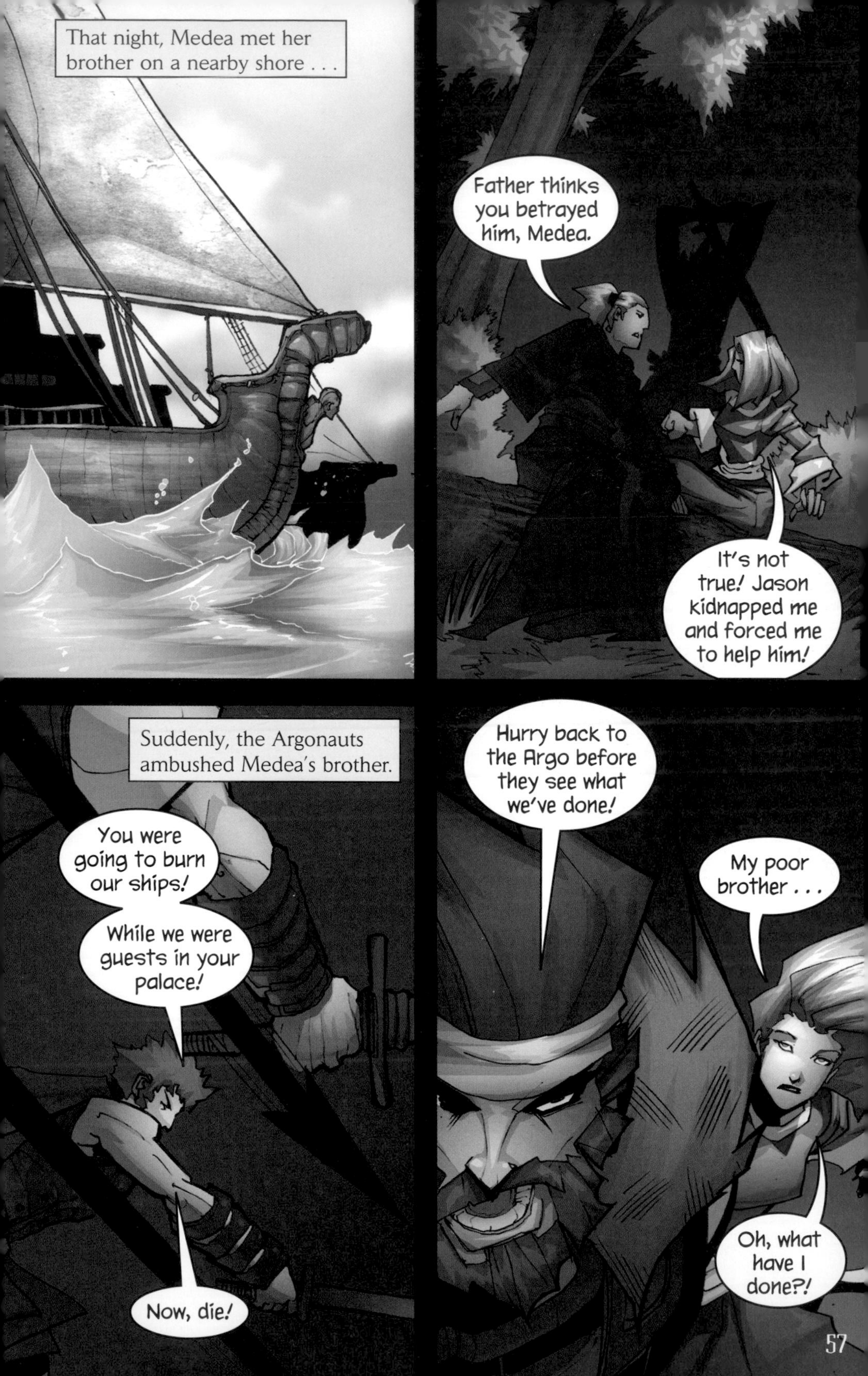

That night, Medea met her brother on a nearby shore . . .
Father thinks you betrayed him, Medea.
It's not true! Jason kidnapped me and forced me to help him!
Suddenly, the Argonauts ambushed Medea's brother.
You were going to burn our ships!
While we were guests in your palace!
Now, die!
Hurry back to the Argo before they see what we've done!
My poor brother . . .
Oh, what have I done?!

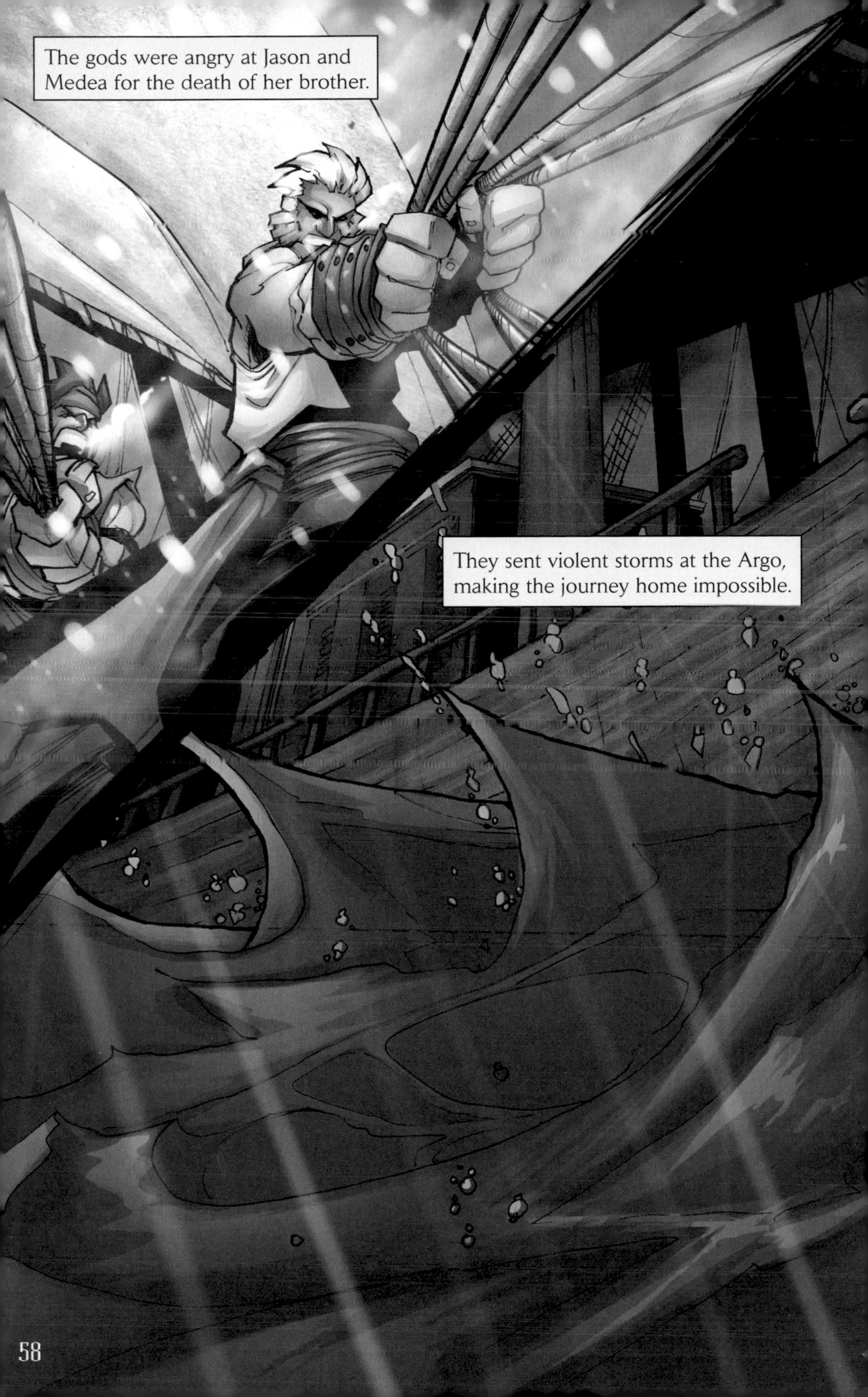
The gods were angry at Jason and Medea for the death of her brother.
They sent violent storms at the Argo, making the journey home impossible.

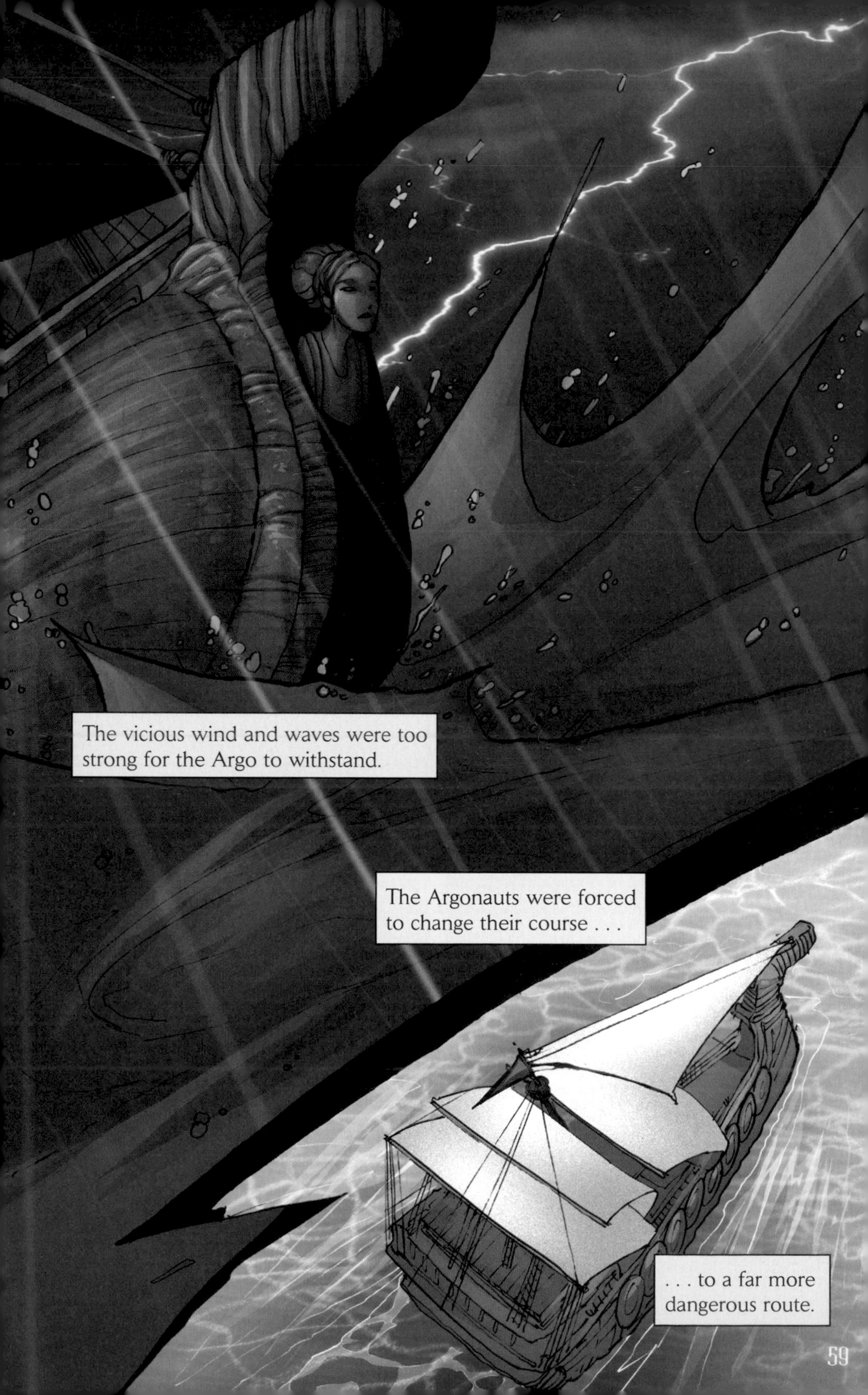
The vicious wind and waves were too strong for the Argo to withstand.
The Argonauts were forced to change their course . . .
. . . to a far more dangerous route.

CHAPTER 6: RECLAIMING THE THRONE

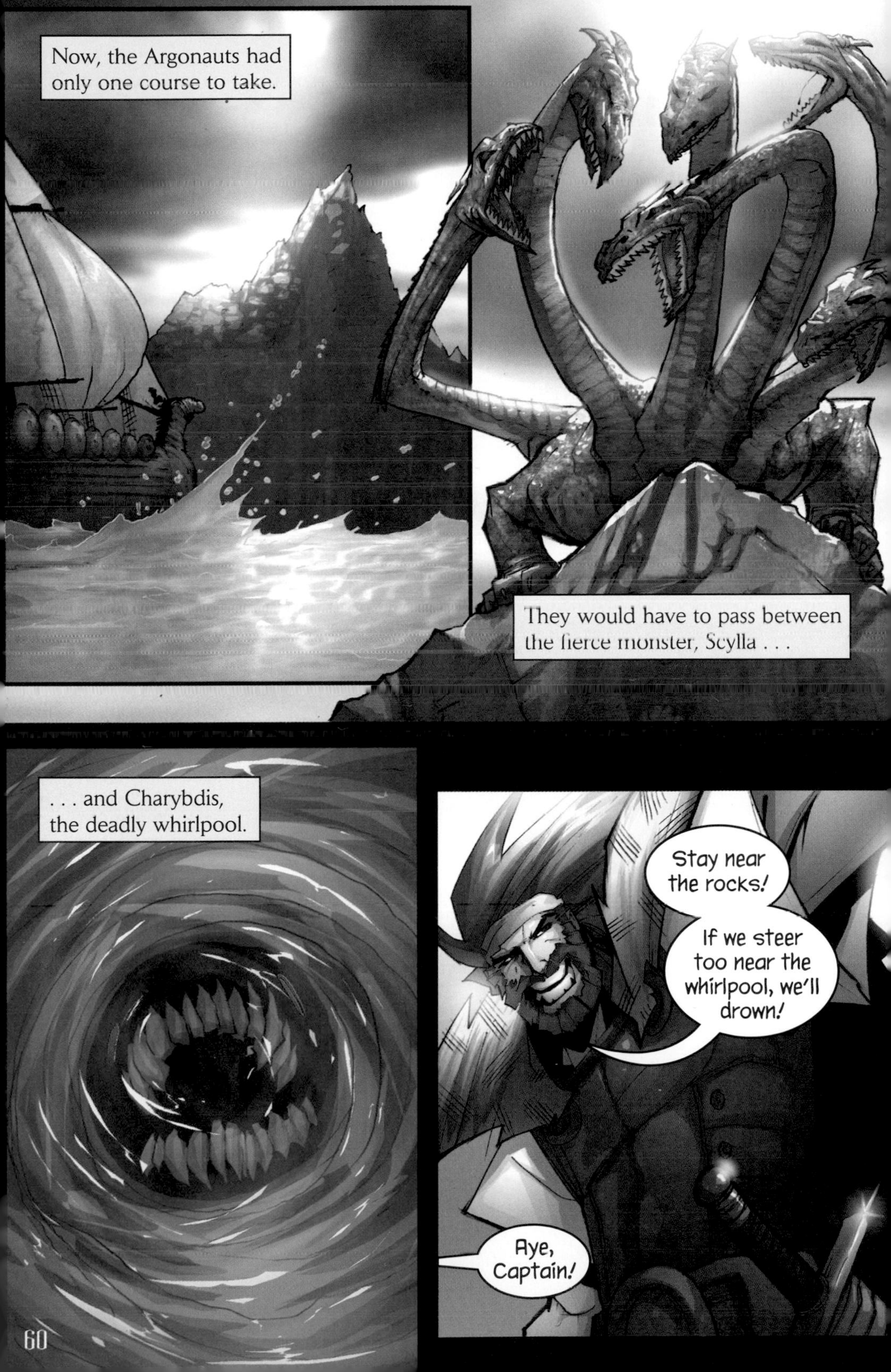

Now, the Argonauts had only one course to take.

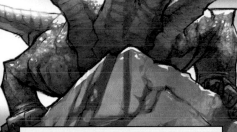

They would have to pass between the fierce monster, Scylla . . .

. . . and Charybdis, the deadly whirlpool.

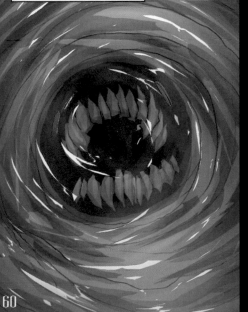

Stay near the rocks!

If we steer too near the whirlpool, we'll drown!

Aye, Captain!

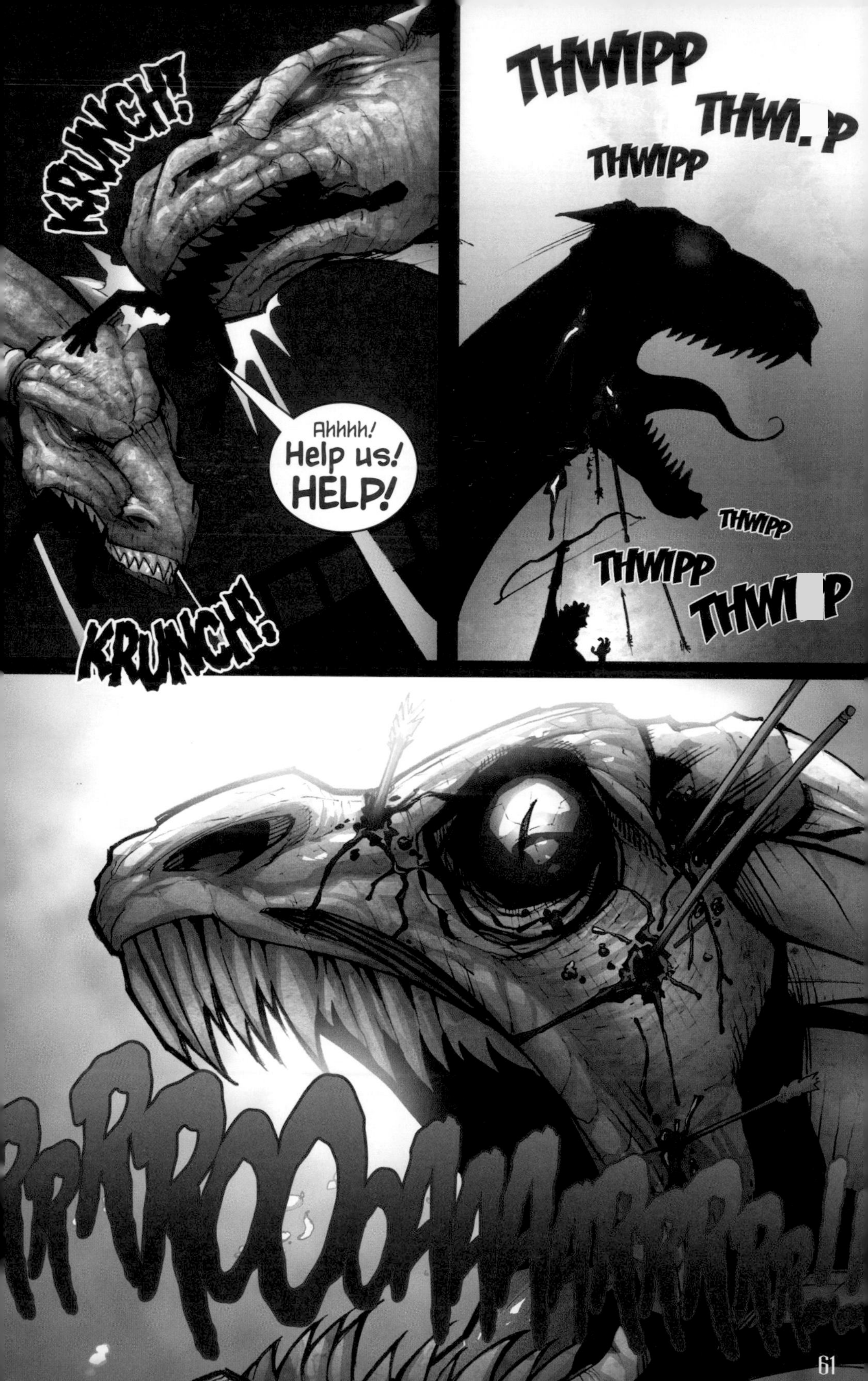
KRUNCH!
Ahhhh!
Help us!
HELP!
KRUNCH!
THWIPP
THWIPP
THWIPP
THWIPP
RRROOAAARRRRR!!

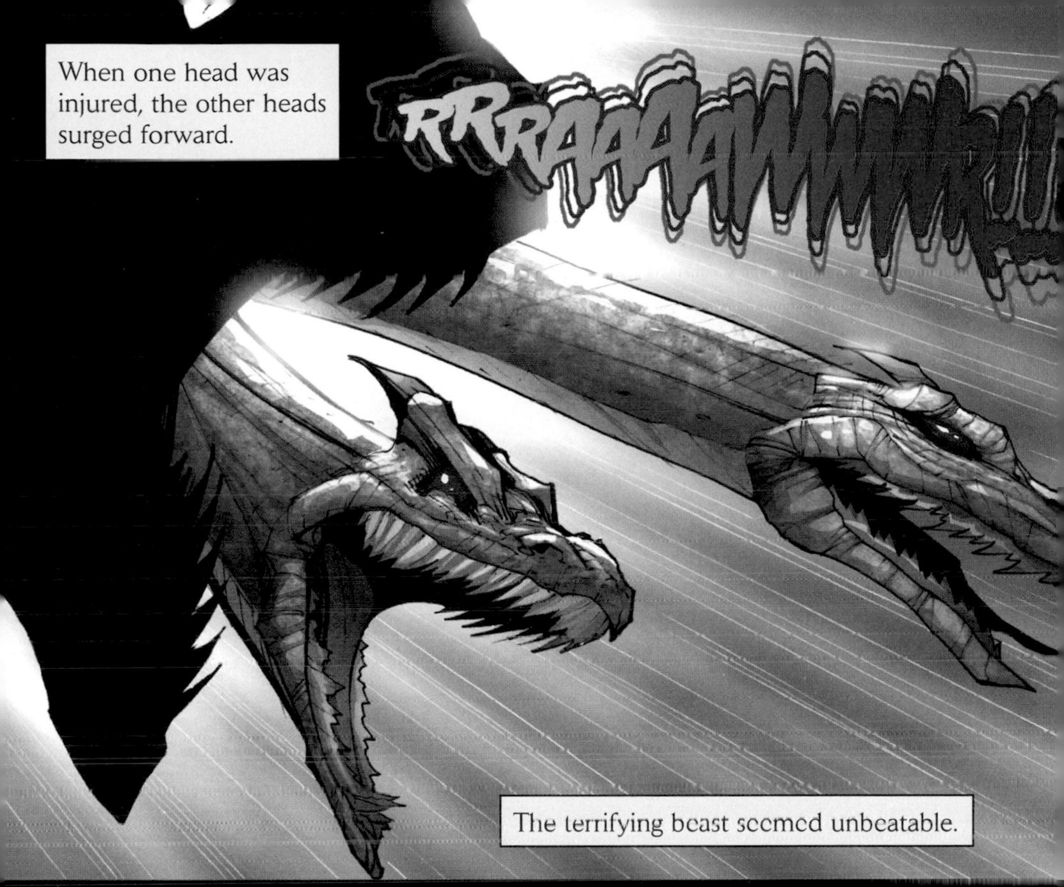
When one head was injured, the other heads surged forward.
RRRAAAAWWWRR
The terrifying beast seemed unbeatable.

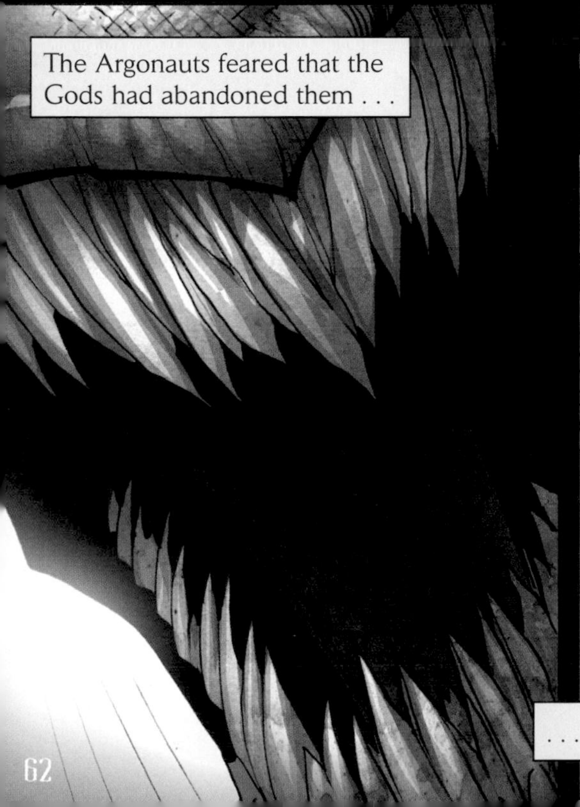
The Argonauts feared that the Gods had abandoned them . . .

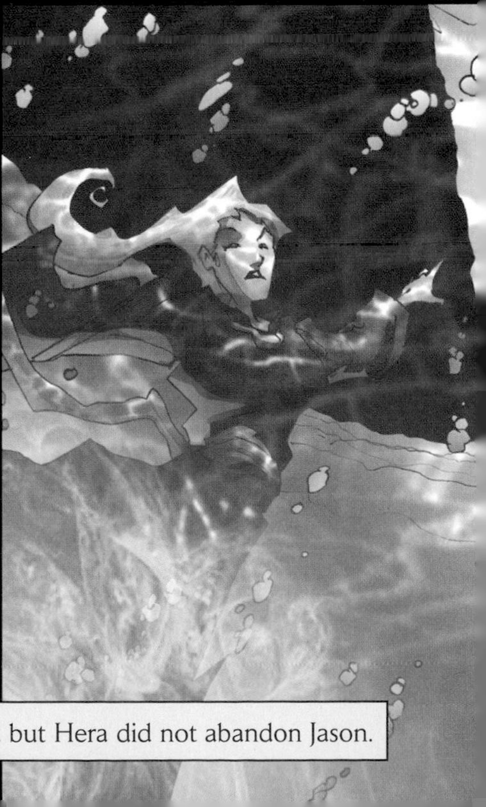
. . . but Hera did not abandon Jason.

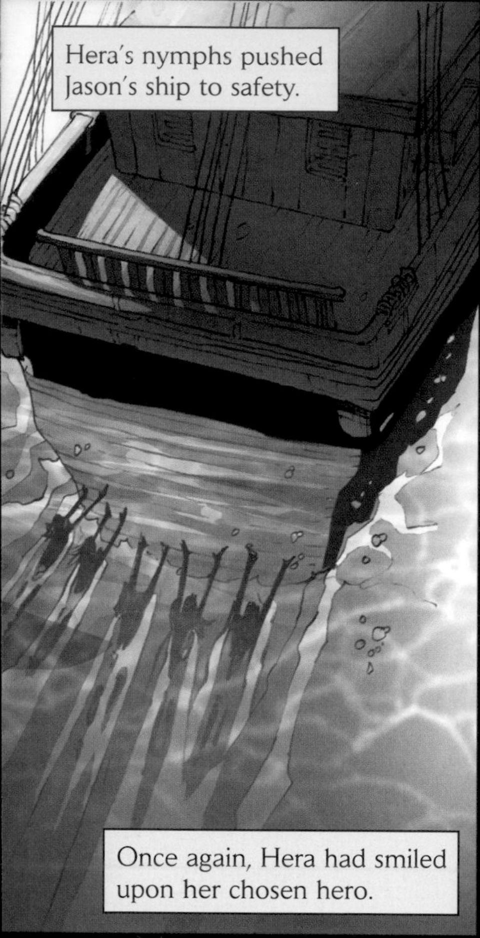
Hera's nymphs pushed Jason's ship to safety.
Once again, Hera had smiled upon her chosen hero.
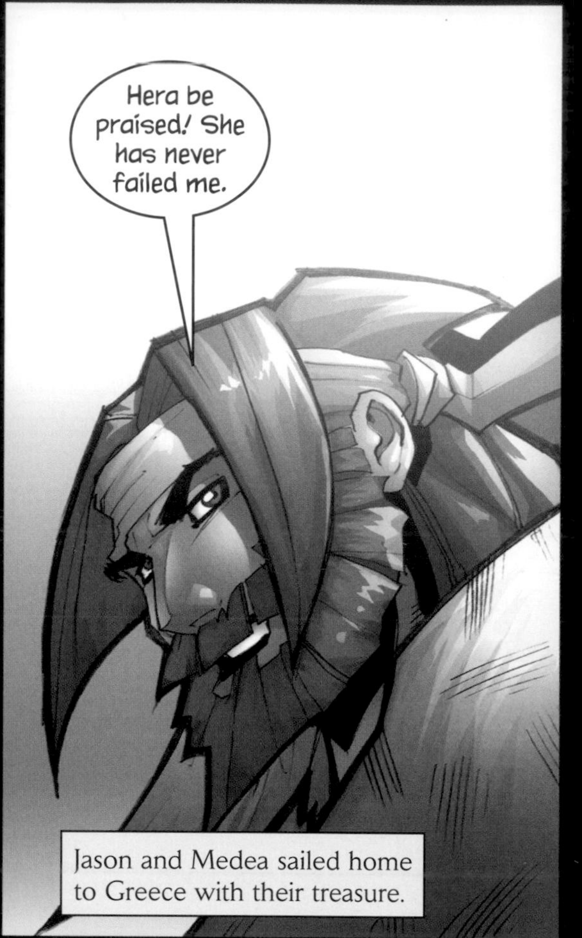
Hera be praised! She has never failed me.
Jason and Medea sailed home to Greece with their treasure.
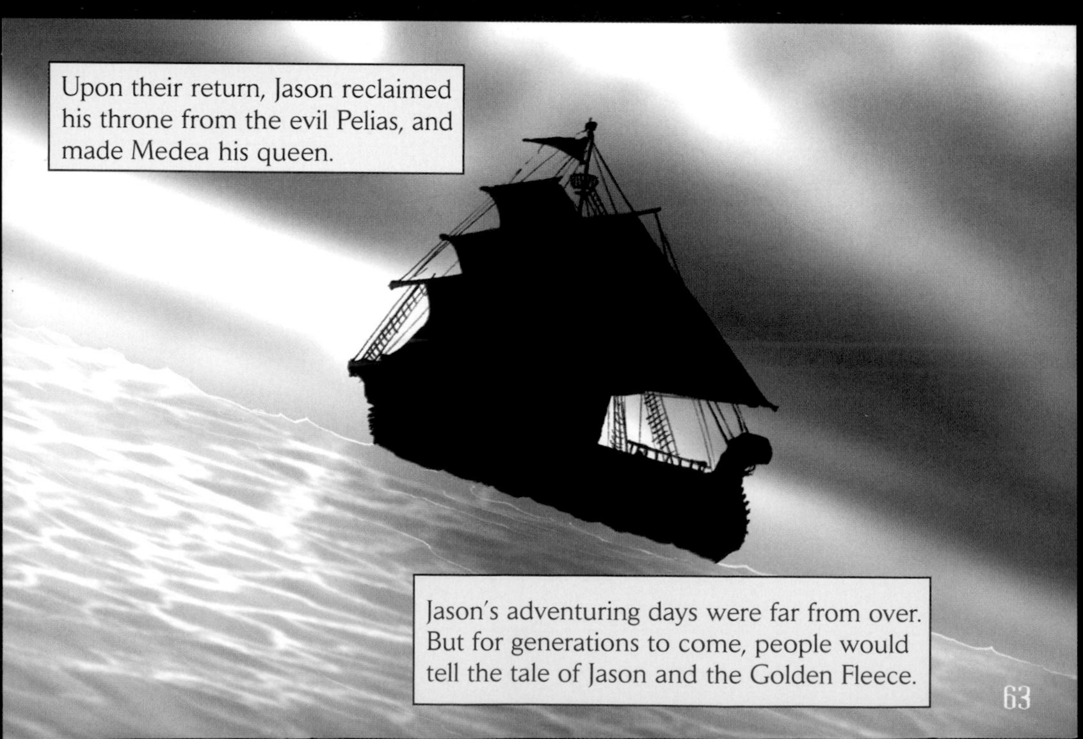
Upon their return, Jason reclaimed his throne from the evil Pelias, and made Medea his queen.
Jason's adventuring days were far from over. But for generations to come, people would tell the tale of Jason and the Golden Fleece.

ABOUT THE RETELLING AUTHOR

The career path of Nel Yomtov has taken him from the halls of Marvel Comics, as an editor, writer, and colorist, to the world of toy development. He then became editorial and art director at a children's nonfiction book publisher, and now Nel is a writer and editor of books, websites, and comics for children. A harmonica-honking blues enthusiast, Nel lives in New York with his wife, Nancy. They have a son, Jess.

ABOUT THE ILLUSTRATOR

Gerardo Sandoval is a professional comic book illustrator from Mexico. He has worked on many well-known comics including *Tomb Raider* books from Top Cow Production. He has also worked on designs for posters and card sets.

GLOSSARY

abandon (uh-BAN-duhn)—leave forever or give up

betray (bi-TRAY)—to be disloyal to someone

clashing (KLASH-ing)—crashing together

deserted (di-ZURT-id)—empty or abandoned

figurehead (FIG-yur-hed)—a carved figure built into the front of a sailing ship

fleece (FLEES)—coat of wool that covers a sheep or ram

inherit (in-HAYR-it)—receive something that is passed down from someone who has died

nymph (NIMF)—a female spirit or goddess who is closely related to nature

strait (STRAYT)—a narrow strip of water that connects two larger bodies of water

THE STRENGTH OF THE MIND

Jason and his Argonauts faced many threats during their voyage. While the crew had many of the world's most powerful warriors, not all of the threats they faced could be solved by strength alone.

During the journey, the Argonauts came across three half-bird, half-human females called the Sirens, who lived on an isolated and rocky island. When ships would sail by, the Sirens sang their hypnotic songs, distracting the sailors and causing their ships to crash into jagged rocks. When the Argo sailed by, the Sirens began to hypnotize Jason and his men, but Orpheus, a simple musician, recognized the danger. He took out his lyre, a stringed instrument, and played it as loud as he could in order to drown out the Sirens' song. Orpheus single-handedly saved the Argonauts without so much as raising a fist.

The Argonauts once sought shelter on the island of Crete. However, the island was guarded by a gigantic bronze man named Talos, who hurled large rocks as ships came ashore. The mighty Argonauts had no idea how to defeat the metal monster, but Medea discovered Talos's one weakness: a vein at the base of his heel, sealed shut with a bronze nail. Medea cast a spell on Talos to calm him. When she removed the bronze nail, Talos bled to death.

GREEK MYTHS TODAY

Greek myths have influenced popular culture across the world for ages. Nowadays, many organizations use ancient Greek myths, gods, and heroes to represent their causes.

An organization called the JASON project was founded in 1989 by the man who discovered the famous RMS *Titanic* wreckage, Dr. Robert D. Ballard. The program gets kids interested in science by using television to broadcast live science adventures, like deep-sea dives and the exploration of active volcanoes. Dr. Ballard chose Jason's name for the program because Jason, accompanied by his Argonauts, journeyed fearlessly across water and land in the name of good. He explored areas of the world that few others had ever seen.

DISCUSSION QUESTIONS

1. Jason and Medea fall in love at first sight — with a little help from Cupid, of course. Do you believe in love at first sight? Why or why not?

2. Jason had a lot of help during his voyage. Who do you think helped him the most? Why?

3. Jason uses his muscles, and his brains, to overcome his enemies. Which do you think is more important — power or intelligence? Why?

WRITING PROMPTS

1. Phineas the prophet was punished for telling the future. Pretend that you can predict the future. What will you do with your newfound skills? Write about it.

2. Imagine that you're an Argonaut like Jason. What kinds of adventures would you have? Who would your crew members be? Write about an adventure of yours.

3. There were lots of monsters and creatures in Jason's adventures. Pretend that Jason encounters one more monster. What is its name? What does it look like? Write a short story about the battle. Then, draw a picture of the creature.

OTHER BOOKS

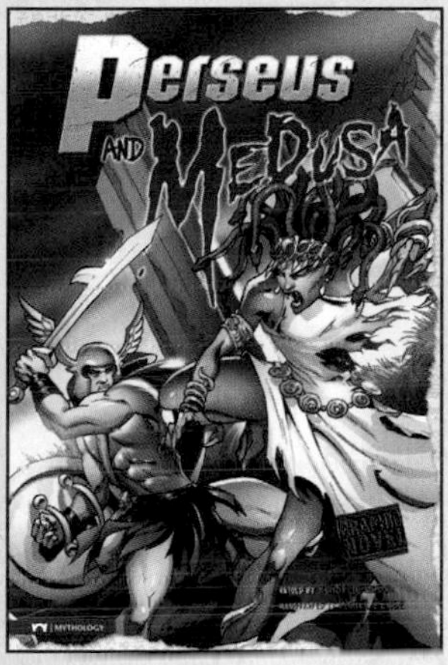
Perseus
AND
Medusa

Perseus and Medusa

Young Perseus grows up, unaware of his royal birth. Before he can claim his heritage, the hero is ordered to slay a hideous monster named Medusa, whose gaze turns men into solid stone. How can the youth fight an enemy he cannot even look at?

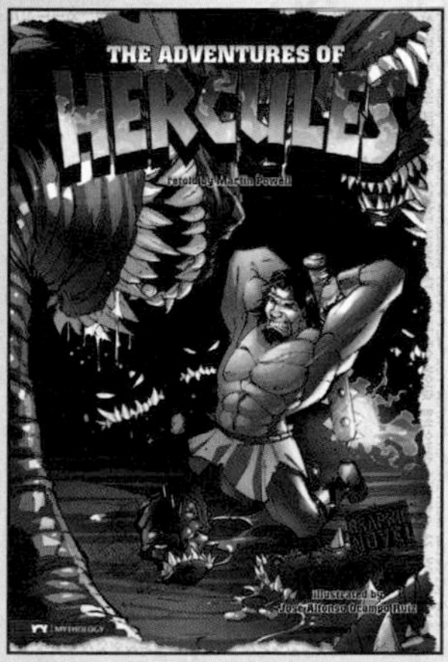
THE ADVENTURES OF
HERCULES

The Adventures of Hercules

Born of a mortal woman and the king of the gods, Hercules is blessed with extraordinary strength. The goddess Hera commands that the mighty Hercules must undergo twelve incredible tasks to pay for a mistake he made in the past.

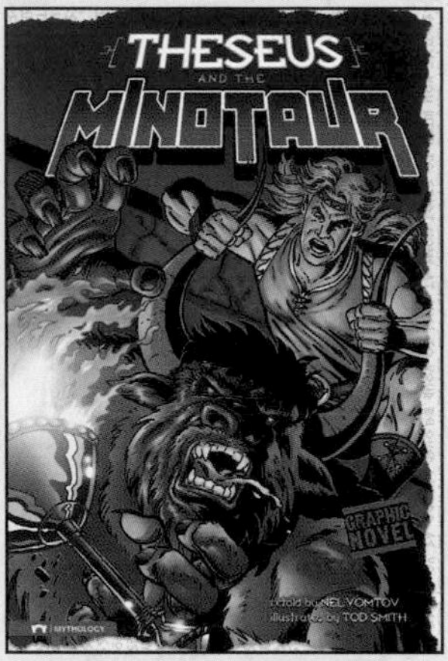
THESEUS
AND THE
MINOTAUR
GRAPHIC NOVEL
retold by NEL YOMTOV
illustrated by TOD SMITH
MYTHOLOGY

Theseus and the Minotaur

The evil king of Crete demands that fourteen young Athenians be fed to the Minotaur, a half-man, half-bull. Only Prince Theseus can save them from the fearsome monster that lives deep in the maze-like Labyrinth.

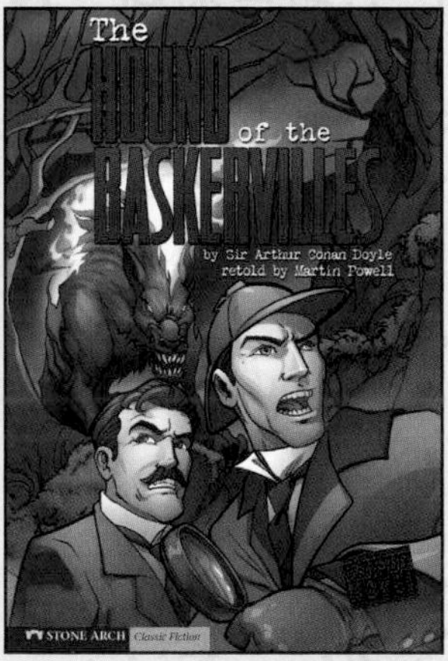
The
HOUND
of the
BASKERVILLES
by Sir Arthur Conan Doyle
retold by Martin Powell
STONE ARCH Classic Fiction

The Hound of the Baskervilles

Late one night, Sir Charles Baskerville is attacked outside his castle in Dartmoor, England. Could it be the Hound of the Baskervilles, a legendary creature that haunts the nearby moor? Sherlock Holmes, the world's greatest detective, is on the case.

SITES

Do you want to know more about subjects related to this book? Or are you interested in learning about other topics? Then check out FactHound, a fun, easy way to find Internet sites.

Our investigative staff has already sniffed out great sites for you!

Here's how to use FactHound:

1. Visit www.facthound.com

2. Select your grade level.

3. To learn more about subjects related to this book, type in the book's ISBN number: **9781434211729**.

4. Click the **Fetch It** button.

FactHound will fetch the best Internet sites for you!